【英译文】

In the Chen State supplies fell short and his followers became so weak that they could not drag themselves on to their feet. Zi Lu came to the Master and said indignantly, "Is it right that even a gentleman should be reduced to the last extremity?" The Master said, "A gentleman withstands hardships, but when petty men are so reduced they lose all self-control."

15.3

子曰："赐也[1]，女以予为多学而识之者与[2]？"对曰："然。非与？"曰："非也，予一以贯之[3]。"

【中译文】

孔子说："子贡呀，你以为我是多学博闻而牢记的人吗？"子贡答说："是的。不是这样吗？"孔子说："不是的。我的学说有一个内在的统一性的。"

【注释】

1 赐：端木赐，字子贡。

2 女：同"汝"。你。

3 以：用。一：一个基本的原则、思想。孔子这里指的是"忠恕"之道。贯：贯穿，贯通。

【英译文】

The Master (Confucius) said, Zi Gong ,I believe you refer to me as one whose aim is simply to learn and retain in mind as many things as possible. Zi Gong replied, That is what I thought. Is it not so? The Master said, No, I have

one (thread) upon which I string them all.

15.4

子曰："由，知德者鲜矣[1]。"

【中译文】

孔子说："仲由，懂得道德的人少啊。"

【注释】

1 鲜（xiǎn）：少。

【英译文】

The Master (Confucius) said, Zhong You those who understand moral force are indeed few.

15.5

子曰："无为而治者[1]，其舜也与？夫何为哉？恭己正南面而已矣[2]。"

【中译文】

孔子说："无为而使天下得到治理的，大概只有虞舜吧？他做了些什么呢？他只是内在谦恭地治理天下罢了。"

【注释】

1 无为而治："无为"，无所作为。据传，舜当政时，

一切沿袭尧的旧法来治国，似乎没有什么新的改变和作为，而使天下太平。后泛指以德化民，无事于政刑。朱熹《四书集注》说："圣人德盛而民化，不待其有所作为也。独称舜者，绍尧之后，而又得人以任众 职，故尤不见有为之迹也。"

2 南面：古代传统礼法，王位总是坐北朝南的。

【英译文】

The Master (Confucius) said, Among those that 'ruled by inactivity' surely Shun may be counted. For what action did he take? He merely placed himself gravely and reverently with his face due south; that was all.

15.6

子张问行，子曰："言忠信，行笃敬，虽蛮貊之邦[1]，行矣。言不忠信，行不笃敬，虽州里[2]，行乎哉？立则见其参于前也[3]，在舆则见其倚于衡也[4]，夫然后行。"子张书诸绅[5]。

【中译文】

子张问行为的准则。孔子说："说话忠诚守信，行为敦厚恭敬，即使在蛮貊地区，也行得通。说话不忠信，行为不笃敬，即使在本乡州里，能行得通吗？'忠信笃敬'这几个字，站着，仿佛看见它直立在眼前；坐车，仿佛看见它依靠在车辕的横木上。这样做了以后

就能行得通。"子张把孔子的话写在自己的衣带上。

【注释】

1 蛮：南蛮，泛指南方边疆少数民族。貊（mò）：北狄，泛指北方边疆少数民族。

2 州里：古代两千五百家为州。五家为邻，五邻为里。这里代指本乡本土。

3 参：本意为直、高。这里引申为像一个高大的东西直立在眼前。

4 舆（yú）：车。倚：依靠在物体或人身上。衡：车辕前的横木。

5 书诸绅：即"书之于绅。""绅"，系在腰间下垂的宽大的衣带。把警句、格言写在腰间的大带子上，一低头就能看到，从而时时提醒自己，指导自己的言行。这是古人一种加强自我修养的方法。

【英译文】

Zi Zhang asked about getting on with people. The Master said, Be loyal and true to your every word, serious and careful in all you do; and you will get on well enough, even though you find yourself among barbarians. But if you are disloyal and untrustworthy in your speech, frivolous and careless in your acts, even though you are among your own neighbours, how can you hope to get on well? When standing, see these principles ranged before you; in your carriage, see them resting on the yoke. Then you may be sure that you will get on. Zi Zhang wrote this down on his sash.

15.7

子曰："直哉史鱼[1]！邦有道如矢，邦无道如矢。君子哉蘧伯玉[2]！邦有道则仕，邦无道则可卷而怀之。"

【中译文】

孔子说："正直啊史鱼！国家政治清明时他像箭一样刚直；国家黑暗时，也像箭头一样刚直。蘧伯玉真是一位君子啊！国家政治清明时出来做官；国家黑暗时，则隐藏起来辞官隐居。"

【注释】

1 史鱼：卫国大夫，名鰌（qiū），字子鱼。他曾多次向卫灵公推荐贤臣蘧伯玉，未被采纳。史鱼病危临终时，嘱咐儿子，不要"治丧正堂"，用这种做法再次劝告卫灵公一定要进用蘧伯玉，而贬斥奸臣弥子瑕。等卫灵公采纳实行之后，才"从丧北堂成礼。"史鱼这种正直的行为，被古人称为"尸谏"（事见《孔子家语》及《韩诗外传》）。

2 蘧伯玉：参见《宪问篇第十四》第二十五章注。

【英译文】

The Master (Confucius) said, Straight and upright indeed was the recorder Shi Yu! When the Way prevailed in the land he was (straight) as an arrow; when the Way ceased to prevail, he was (straight) as an arrow. A gentleman

indeed is Qu Boyu. When the Way prevailed in his land, he served the State; but when the Way ceased to prevail, he knew how to 'wrap it up and hide it in the folds of his dress'.

15.8

子曰："可与言而不与之言，失人；不可与言而与之言，失言。知者不失人[1]，亦不失言。"

【中译文】

孔子说："可以与他说却不与他说，就会失交于人；不可与他说却与他说，就是言语不慎。聪明人既不失交于人，也不言语不慎。"

【注释】

1 知：同"智"。智者，聪明人。

【英译文】

The Master (Confucius) said, Not to talk to one who could be talked to, is to lose a man. To talk to those who cannot be talked to, is to waste one's words. 'He who is truly wise never loses a man'; but on the other hand, he never wastes his words.

15.9

子曰："志士仁人，无求生以害仁[1]，有杀身以成仁[2]。"

【中译文】

孔子说："有志之士，仁义之人，不会为求保命而损害仁，而会献出生命以保全仁。"

【注释】

1 求生：贪生怕死，为保活命苟且偷生。

2 杀身：勇于自我牺牲，为仁义当死而死，心安德全。

【英译文】

The Master (Confucius) said, Neither the knight who has truly the heart of a knight nor the man of good stock who has the qualities that belong to good stock will ever seek life at the expense of Goodness; and it may be that he has to give his life in order to achieve Goodness.

15.10

子贡问为仁，子曰："工欲善其事[1]，必先利其器[2]。居是邦也，事其大夫之贤者[3]，友其士之仁者。"

【中译文】

子贡问怎样推行仁德。孔子说："工匠要把活儿干好，必先磨锐工具。住在一个国家，就要事奉大夫中有贤德的人，与有仁德的知识分子交朋友。"

【注释】

1 善：用作动词。做好，干好，使其完善。

2 利：用作动词。搞好，弄好，使其精良。

3 事：事奉，为……服务。

【英译文】

Zi Gong asked how to become Good. The Master said, A craftsman, if he means to do good work, must first sharpen his tools. In whatever State you live, take service with such of its officers as are worthy and make friends with such of its knights as are Good.

15.11

颜渊问为邦[1]，子曰："行夏之时[2]，乘殷之辂[3]，服周之冕[4]，乐则《韶》《舞》[5]，放郑声[6]，远佞人[7]。郑声淫，佞人殆[8]。"

【中译文】

颜渊问怎样建设国家。孔子说："遵行夏代的历法，驾乘殷代的车子，戴周代的礼帽，奏《韶》乐、《舞》乐，禁止郑国的乐曲，疏远花言巧语的小人。郑国的乐曲不正派，花言巧语的小人危险。"

【注释】

1 为：建设，治理。邦：邦国，诸侯国。

2 夏之时："时"，时令，时节。此指历法。夏之时，就是沿用至今的夏历（又称阴历，农历）。周历建子（以夏历十一月为正月），殷历建丑（以夏历十

15.12

子曰："人无远虑，必有近忧[1]。"

【中译文】

孔子说："人没有长远打算，必定会有眼前的忧愁。"

【注释】

1 远，近：指时间。犹言未来，目前。一说，指地方。朱熹说："人之所履者，容足之外，皆为无用之地，而不可废也。故虑不在千里之外，则患在几席之下矣。"

【英译文】

The Master (Confucius) said, The man who will not worry about what is far off will soon find something worse than worry close at hand.

15.13

子曰："已矣乎，吾未见好德如好色者也[1]。"

【中译文】

孔子说："罢了啊，我没见过喜欢德行像喜欢美色那样的人。"

【注释】

1 本章文字与《子罕篇第九》第十八章略同，可参阅。

二月为正月），夏历建寅（以建寅之月的朔日为岁首），而夏 历最合于农时，有利于农业生产，故孔子主张推行夏历。

3 乘殷之辂："辂（lù）"，古代的大车。旧说殷代的大车木质而无饰，最俭朴实用，故孔子提倡"乘殷之辂"。

4 服周之冕："冕"，礼帽。旧说周代的礼帽体制完备而华美，而孔子是一向提倡礼服应讲究、华美的，故说要"服周之冕。"

5 韶：舜时音乐。舞：同《武》。周武王时音乐。参阅《八佾篇第三》第二十五章注。

6 放：驱逐，排斥，禁止。郑声：郑国的民间音乐。郑国民间音乐形式活泼，与典雅板滞的古乐有很大不同。孔子难以接受，认为它多靡靡之音，故主张"放郑声"。

7 远：作动词用。疏远。

8 殆：危险。

【英译文】

Yan Yuan asked how to govern a State. The Master said, One would go by the seasons of Xia; as State-coach for the ruler one would use that of Yin, and as head-gear of ceremony wear the Zhou hat. For music one would take as model the Succession Dance, and would do away altogether with the tunes of Zheng; one would also keep clever talkers at a distance. For the tunes of Zheng are licentious and clever talkers are dangerous.

【英译文】

The Master (Confucius) said, I haven't looked for one whose desire to build up his moral power was as strong as sexual desire.

15.14

子曰：“臧文仲其窃位者与[1]？知柳下惠之贤[2]，而不与立也[3]。”

【中译文】

孔子说：“臧文仲大概是个窃据官位的人吧？明知柳下惠是贤人，却不任用他。”

【注释】

1 臧文仲：即臧孙辰。鲁国大夫，历仕鲁庄公、鲁闵公、鲁僖公、鲁文公四朝。知贤而不举，故孔子批评他“不仁”，“窃位”。参见《公冶长篇第五》第十八章注。窃位：窃据高位，占有官位而不称职、不尽责。

2 柳下惠：本姓展，名获，字禽，又名展季。他的封地（一说是居处）叫“柳下”；死后，由他的妻子倡议，给他的“私谥”（并非由朝廷授予的谥号）叫“惠”，故称“柳下惠”。春秋中期的贤者，鲁国大夫，曾任“士师”（掌管刑狱的官员）。以讲究礼节而著称。

3 与立：即“与之并立于朝”，给予官位。一说，“立”同“位”。“与立”，即“与位”。

【英译文】

The Master (Confucius) said, Surely one would not be wrong in calling Zang Wenzhong a stealer of other men's ranks? He knew that Liuxia Hui was the best man for the post, yet would not have him as his colleague.

15.15

子曰：“躬自厚而薄责于人[1]，则远怨矣[2]。”

【中译文】

孔子说：“自己多责备自己而少责备别人，就可以避开怨恨了。”

【注释】

1 躬自厚：意为责己要重，应多多反省责备自己。“躬”，自身。“厚”，这里指厚责，重责。薄　责于人：意为待人要宽，要行恕道，少挑剔责备别人。“薄责”，轻责，少责备。

2 远：远离，避开。

【英译文】

The Master (Confucius) said, To demand much from oneself and little from others is the way (for a ruler) to banish discontent.

15.16

子曰：“不曰‘如之何，如之何’者[1]，吾

末如之何而已矣[2]。”

【中译文】

孔子说：“不说‘怎么办，怎么办’的人，我也不知怎么办了。”

【注释】

1 如之可：犹言怎么办。孔子这里的意思是：做事一定要经过深思熟虑，多问几个“该怎么办”。因为只有深忧远虑的人，才能真正想出解决问题的好办法。

2 末如之何：犹言没办法。“末”，没。

【英译文】

The Master (Confucius) said, If a man does not continually ask himself 'What am I to do about this, what am I to do about this?' there is no possibility of my doing anything to help him.

15.17

子曰：“群居终日，言不及义，好行小慧，难矣哉！”

【中译文】

孔子说：“大家整天聚在一处，言谈不在道理，好卖弄一点小聪明，对这种人真难教育啊！”

【英译文】

The Master (Confucius) said, Those who are capable of spending a whole day together without ever once discussing questions of right or wrong, but who content themselves with performing petty acts of clemency, are indeed difficult.

15.18

子曰：“君子义以为质[1]，礼以行之，孙以出之[2]，信以成之。君子哉！”

【中译文】

孔子说：“君子以义为根本，以礼来实行义，以谦逊的语言来表达义，以诚实的态度来完成义，这就是君子啊！”

【注释】

1 质：本意为本质、质地。引申为基本原则，根本。

2 孙：同“逊”。出：出言，表达。

【英译文】

The Master (Confucius) said, The gentleman who takes justice as his material to work upon and ritual as the guide in putting what is right into practice, who is modest in setting out his projects and faithful in carrying them to their conclusion, he indeed is a true gentleman.

15.19

子曰："君子病无能焉[1]，不病人之不己知也。"

【中译文】

孔子说："君子只担心没有才能，不担心别人不知道自己。"

【注释】

1 病：担心，忧虑。

【英译文】

The Master (Confucius) said, A gentleman is distressed by his own lack of capacity; he is never distressed at the failure of others to recognize his merits.

15.20

子曰："君子疾没世而名不称焉[1]。"

【中译文】

孔子说："君子就怕死后没有好的名声被人称颂。"

【注释】

1 病：恨，怕，感到遗憾。没世：终身，死。称：称述，称道。

【英译文】

The Master (Confucius) said, A gentleman has reason to be distressed if he dies without making a reputation for himself.

15.21

子曰："君子求诸己[1]，小人求诸人。"

【中译文】

孔子说："君子要求自己，小人要求别人。"

【注释】

1 求：要求。一说，求助，求得。则此章意为：君子一切求之于自己，小人一切求之于他人。

【英译文】

The Master (Confucius) said, The demands that a gentleman makes are upon himself; those that a petty man makes are upon others.

15.22

子曰："君子矜而不争[1]，群而不党[2]。"

【中译文】

孔子说："君子庄重矜持而不同别人争执，合群而不结党营私。"

【注释】

1 矜（jīn）：庄重，矜持，慎重拘谨。

2 党：结党营私，拉帮结伙，搞小宗派。

【英译文】

The Master (Confucius) said, A gentleman is dignified, but not quarrelsome, allies himself with individuals, but not with parties.

15.23

子曰："君子不以言举人，不以人废言。"

【中译文】

孔子说："君子不仅仅根据言论选拔人，也不因人有缺点而否定他的言论。"

【英译文】

The Master (Confucius) said, A gentleman does not accept men because of what they say, nor reject sayings, because the speaker is what he is.

15.24

子贡问曰："有一言而可以终身行之者乎？"子曰："其'恕'乎！己所不欲，勿施于人。"

【中译文】

子贡问道："有一句话可以终身奉行的吗？"孔子说："那就是'恕'吧！自己不愿意的，不要强加给别人。"

【英译文】

Zi Gong asked, Is there any single saying that one can act upon all day and every day? The Master said, Perhaps the saying about consideration: 'Never do to others what you would not like them to do to you .'

15.25

子曰："吾之于人也，谁毁谁誉[1]？如有所誉者，其有所试矣。斯民也，三代之所以直道而行也[2]。"

【中译文】

孔子说："我对于别人，诋毁过谁？赞誉过谁？如有所赞誉，那是经过实践考验过的。这些人都是夏商周三代能按正直之道行事的。"

【注释】

1 毁：诋毁。指称人之恶而失其真。誉：赞誉，溢美。指扬人之善而过其实。

2 "斯民也"句："斯"，此，如此。"民"，指用民。"三代"，指夏、商、周。此句是说如此用民，无所偏私，这就是三代能按正直之道行事的原因。

【英译文】

The Master (Confucius) said, In speaking of the men of the day I have always refrained from praise and blame alike. But if there is indeed anyone whom I have praised, there is a means by which he may be tested. For the common people here round us are just such stuff as the three dynasties (Xia, shang,Zhou,)worked upon in the days when they followed the Straight Way.

15.26

子曰："吾犹及史之阙文也[1]，有马者借人乘之[2]。今亡矣夫。"

【中译文】

孔子说："我还能看到史官存疑的阙文，有马的人把马借给别人骑。今天没有了啊。"

【注释】

1 史之阙文："阙"，同"缺"。指缺疑，存疑。史官记载历史，对于有疑问（缺乏确凿根据）的事，缺而不录，抱存疑态度，故有"阙文"。一说，写史的书吏，遇到可疑的字，存疑待问，宁可把缺少的字空起来，也不创造新字，不妄以己意另写别的字来代替。

2 借：借出，把自己的东西暂时给别人使用。句意为：有马的人不敢自私，而愿借给别人骑。一说，"借"，借助。句意为：有马的人，不会驾驭（训练）自己的马，而借助善驯马的人来调习训练。"史阙文"与"马借人"这两句话，看来意义不够连贯。有的学者推

测"有马者"句可能是衍文；也有的学者认为，这两件事均说明古人淳厚朴实，与孔子时的人情浇薄不同，故孔子伤叹。可参。

【英译文】

The Master (Confucius) said, I can still remember the days when a scribe left blank spaces, and when someone using a horse(for the first time) hired a man to drive it. But that is all over now!

15.27

子曰："巧言乱德。小不忍则乱大谋。"

【中译文】

孔子说："花言巧语会败坏道德。小事上不忍耐就会坏了大事。"

【英译文】

The Master (Confucius) said, Clever talk may confound the workings of moral force, just as small impatiences may confound great projects.

15.28

子曰："众恶之，必察焉；众好之，必察焉。"

【中译文】

孔子说："大家都厌恶他，一定要仔细考察原因；大家都喜欢他，一定要仔细考察原因。"

【英译文】

The Master (Confucius) said, When everyone dislikes a man, enquiry is necessary; when everyone likes a man, enquiry is also necessary.

15.29

子曰："人能弘道[1]，非道弘人。"

【中译文】

孔子说："人能够弘扬道，不是道能弘扬人。"

【注释】

1 弘（hóng）：弘扬，光大。

【英译文】

The Master (Confucius) said, A man can develop his Way; but there is no Way that can develop a man.

15.30

子曰："过而不改，是谓过矣。"

【中译文】

孔子说："犯了错误而不改，这才真叫做错误呢。"

【英译文】

The Master (Confucius) said, To have faults and to make no effort to amend them is to have faults indeed!

15.31

子曰："吾尝终日不食，终夜不寝，以思，无益，不如学也。"

【中译文】

孔子说："我曾经整天地不吃饭，整夜地不睡觉，去冥思苦想，结果没有什么益处，还不如去学习呢。"

【英译文】

The Master (Confucius) said, It was no use spending a whole day without food and a whole night without sleep in order to meditate. It is better to learn.

15.32

子曰："君子谋道不谋食。耕也，馁在其中矣[1]；学也，禄在其中矣[2]。君子忧道不忧贫。"

【中译文】

孔子说："君子谋求道，而不是为了谋求衣食。耕田，未必不挨饿；学习知识，则可以获得俸禄。君子担忧道没学好，不担忧贫穷。"

【注 释】

1 馁：饥饿。

2 禄：做官的俸禄。

【英译文】

The Master (Confucius) said, A gentleman's aim is to think of the Way; he does not think how he is going to make a living. Even farming sometimes entails times of shortage; and even learning may incidentally lead to high pay. But a gentleman's anxieties concern the progress of the Way; he has no anxiety concerning poverty.

15.33

子曰："知及之[1]，仁不能守之，虽得之，必失之。知及之，仁能守之，不庄以莅之[2]，则民不敬。知及之，仁能守之，庄以莅之，动之不以礼[3]，未善也。"

【中译文】

孔子说："依靠聪明得到，如果不能用仁德去守住，虽然得到，也一定会失去它。依靠聪明得到，能够用仁德去守住，但如不用庄重严肃的态度去认真对待百姓，百姓也不会敬服。依靠聪明才智得到的，能用仁德去守住它，又能用庄重严肃的态度去认真对待，但是行动不符合礼义，也不能算是尽善的。"

【注 释】

1 知：同"智"。聪明，才智。

2 莅（lì）：到，临。这里指临民，即掌握政权，治理百姓。

3 动之："动"，行动。"之"，语助词，无义。

孔子认为，治理天下，智、仁、庄、礼，四者缺一不可，只用智，其失在荡；只用仁，其失在宽；只用庄，其失在猛；所以必须用礼来调和。

【英译文】

The Master (Confucius) said, He whose wisdom brings him into power, needs Goodness to secure that power. Else, though he get it , he will certainly lose it. He whose wisdom brings him into power and who has Goodness whereby to secure that power, if he has not dignity wherewith to approach the common people, they will not respect him. He whose wisdom has brought him into power, who has Goodness whereby to secure that power and dignity wherewith to approach the common people, if he handle them contrary to the prescriptions of ritual, is not a wonderful ruler.

15.34

子曰："君子不可小知而可大受也[1]，小人不可大受而可小知也。"

【中译文】

孔子说："不可让君子只做小事情，而可让他接受

重大任务；不可让小人接受重大任务，而可让他做些小事情。”

【注释】

1 小知：“知”，主持，主管。小知，即任用做小事情，管小范围内的具体事务。一说，“知”，了解，识别。小知，即从小处、从任用做小事情上，去了解、识别。

【英译文】

The Master (Confucius) said, It is wrong for a gentleman to have knowledge of menial matters and proper that he should be entrusted with great responsibilities. It is wrong for a petty man to be entrusted with great responsibilities, but proper that he should have a knowledge of menial matters.

15.35

子曰：“民之于仁也，甚于水火，水火吾见蹈而死者矣，未见蹈仁而死者也[1]。”

【中译文】

孔子说：“老百姓对于仁德，比对水火更迫切需要；但是我见过溺水蹈火而死的，却没见过实践仁德而死的。”

【注释】

1 蹈（dǎo）：踏，踩，投入。引申为追求，实行，实践。朱熹《四书集注》说：“民之于水火，所

赖以生，不可一日无。其于仁也亦然。但水火外物，而仁在己。无水火，不过害人之身，而不仁则失其心。是仁有甚于水火，而尤不可以一日无者也。况水火或有时而杀人，仁则未尝杀人，亦何惮而不为哉？”可见本章精神在于“勉人为仁”。

【英译文】

The Master said, Goodness is more importance to the people than water and fire. I have seen men lose their lives when 'treading upon' water and fire; but I have never seen anyone lose his life through 'treading upon 'Goodness.

15.36

子曰：“当仁不让于师。”

【中译文】

孔子说：“当面对合于仁德的事，即使对老师，也不必谦让。”

【英译文】

The Master (Confucius) said, When it comes to Goodness one need not avoid competing with one's teacher.

15.37

子曰：“君子贞而不谅[1]。”

【中译文】

孔子说："君子坚持正道，而不固守小信。"

【注释】

1 贞：正，固守正道，恪守节操。谅：信，守信用执。本章与孔子所说"言不必信，行不必果"同一意思。可阅《子路篇第十三》第二十章。

【英译文】

The Master (Confucius) said, From a gentleman justice is expected, but not blind fidelity.

15.38

子曰："事君，敬其事而后其食[1]。"

【中译文】

孔子说："侍奉国君，要恭敬谨慎地办事，而把取俸禄的事往后放。"

【注释】

1 食：食禄，俸禄，官吏的薪水。

【英译文】

The Master (Confucius) said, In serving one's prince one should be intent upon the task, not bent upon the pay.

15.39

子曰："有教无类[1]。"

【中译文】

孔子说："对所有人都进行教育，不看出身生而分。"

【注释】

1 无类：不分类，没有富贵贫贱、天资优劣智愚、等级地位高低、地域远近、善恶不同等等的区别与限制。孔子提倡全民教育，希望教育所有的人而同归于善。他的弟子中富有的（如冉有、子贡），贫穷的（如颜回、原思），地位高的（如孟懿子为鲁国贵族），地位低的（如子路为卞之野人），鲁钝一点的（如曾参），愚笨一点的（如高柴），各种人都有。

【英译文】

The Master (Confucius) said, There is a difference in instruction but none in kind.

15.40

子曰："道不同[1]，不相为谋。"

【中译文】

孔子说："思想主张不同，不能互相谋划商讨。"

【注释】

1 道：道路，主张，所追求的目标。

【英译文】

The Master (Confucius) said, Men who are different in their way can't take counsel with each other.

15.41

子曰："辞达而已矣。"

【中译文】

孔子说："言辞足以表达意思就行了。"

【英译文】

The Master (Confucius) said, In official speeches all that matters is to get one's meaning through.

15.42

师冕见[1]，及阶，子曰："阶也。"及席，子曰："席也。"皆坐，子告之曰："某在斯，某在斯。"

师冕出，子张问曰："与师言之道与？"子曰："然，固相师之道也[2]。"

【中译文】

师冕来见孔子，走到台阶边，孔子说："这是台阶。"走到坐席边，孔子说："这是坐席。"大家都坐下后，孔子告诉他说："某某人在这里，某某人在那里。"师冕走了以后，子张问："这就是与乐师讲话的方法吗？"孔子说："是的，此是帮助乐师的方法。"

【注释】

1 师：指乐师。一般是盲人。冕：盲人乐师的名字。

2 相：帮助，辅助。

【英译文】

The Music-master Mian came to see him. When he reached the steps, the Master said, Here are the steps. When he reached the mat, the Master said, Here is the mat. When everyone was seated the Master informed him saying, So-and-so is here, So-and-so is there. When the Music-master Mian had gone,Tzu-chang asked saying, 'Is that the recognized way to talk to a Music-master?' The Master said, Yes, certainly it is the recognized way to help a Music-master.

季氏篇第十六（共十四章）

Confucius Talking about How a Gentleman Act

16.1

季氏将伐颛臾[1]。冉有、季路见于孔子曰[2]：“季氏将有事于颛臾[3]。”

孔子曰：“求，无乃尔是过与[4]？夫颛臾，昔者先王以为东蒙主[5]，且在邦域之中矣，是社稷之臣也[6]。何以伐为[7]？”

冉有曰：“夫子欲之[8]，吾二臣者皆不欲也。”

孔子曰：“求！周任有言曰[9]：‘陈力就列[10]，不能者止。’危而不持，颠而不扶，则将焉用彼相矣[11]？且尔言过矣。虎兕出于柙[12]，龟玉毁于椟中[13]，是谁之过与？”

冉有曰：“今夫颛臾，固而近于费[14]。今不取，后世必为子孙忧。”

孔子曰：“求！君子疾夫舍曰欲之而必为之辞[15]。丘也闻有国有家者，不患贫而患不均，不患寡而患不安[16]。盖均无贫，和无寡，安无倾。夫如是，故远人不服，则修文德以来之[17]。既来之，则安之。今由与求也，相夫子，远人不服，

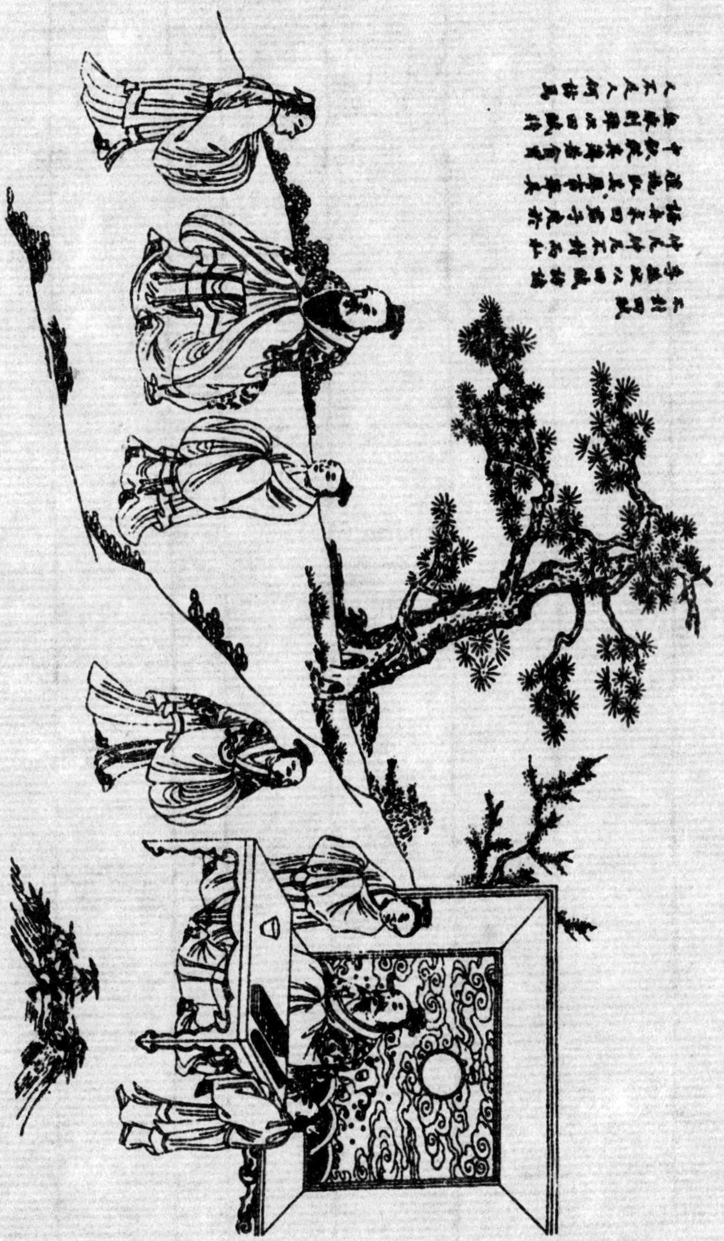

No Answer to the Question about Land Tax

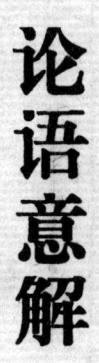

而不能来也；邦分崩离析[18]，而不能守也；而谋动干戈于邦内。吾恐季孙之忧，不在颛臾，而在萧墙之内也[19]。

【中译文】

季氏将要讨伐颛臾。冉有、季路去见孔子说：“季氏准备征讨颛臾。”孔子说：“冉求！这难道不是你的过错吗？颛臾，先王曾经让其主持东蒙山的祭祀，而且就在鲁国境内，是我们鲁国共安危的臣属，为什么要征讨它呢？”冉有说：“季孙大夫想这么做，我们二人作为家臣，都不想这么做。”孔子说：“冉求！周任曾有句话说：‘能够尽自己的才力，就担任职务；实在做不到，就该辞职。’遇到危险不扶持，摔倒了不搀扶，那么，用你这助手做什么呢？而且你的话错了。老虎、犀牛从关它的笼子里跑了出来，贵重的玉器在木匣中被毁坏了，这是谁的过错呢？”冉有说：“如今颛臾城墙坚固，而且离费邑很近。现在不占领它，后世必然成为子孙的祸患。”孔子说：“冉求！君子厌恶那种嘴上不说‘想得到’，却一定要找个借口得到的人。我听说过，对于拥有国家的诸侯和拥有采邑的大夫，不担心贫穷，而是担心分配不均；不担心人少，而是担心社会不安定。因为财富分配均匀了，就无所谓贫穷；国内和睦团结了，就不显得人少势弱；社会安定了，国家就没有倾覆的危险。要是这样做了，远方的人还不归服，便提倡仁义礼乐道德教化，以使他们归附。远方的人已经来了，就使他安心住下来。现在仲由、冉求你们二人辅佐季康子，远处的人不归服，而不能使之归附；国家四分五裂，而不能保全；反而打算在国境之内使用武力。我只怕季孙氏的忧患，不在颛臾，而在自己的家门之内。”

【注释】

1 季氏：即季孙氏，指季康子，名肥。鲁国大夫。颛臾（zhuān yú）：附属于鲁国的一个小国，子爵。故城在今山东省费县西北八十里。

2 冉有，季路：孔子弟子。冉有即冉求，字子有，也称冉有。季路即仲由，字子路，因仕于季氏，又称季路。

3 有事：这里指施加武力，采取军事行动。

4 无乃：岂不是，恐怕是，难道不是。

5 先王：鲁国的始祖周公（姬旦），系周武王（姬发）之弟，故这里称周天子为先王。东蒙主：谓主祭东蒙。“东蒙”，即蒙山。因在鲁国东部，故称东蒙。在今山东省蒙阴县南四十里，与费县连接。“主”，主持祭祀。

6 社稷之臣：国家的重臣。

7 何以伐为：“何以”，以何，为什么。“为”，语气助词。相当于“呢”。为什么要讨伐他呢？

8 夫子：古时对老师、长者、尊贵者的尊称。这里指季康子。

故称“萧墙”。“萧”、“肃”古字通。这里用“萧墙”，借　指宫内。当时鲁国的国君鲁哀公名义上在位，实际上政　权被季康子把持；这样发展下去，一旦鲁君不能容忍，　必起内乱。故孔子含蓄地说了这话　。

【英译文】

When the head of the Ji Family was about to attack the state of Zhuan Yu, Ran You and Zi Lu came to see the Master and said to him, "The head of the Ji Family is about to have an incident with Zhuan Yu."

The Master (Confucius) said, "Ran You, I fear you must be held responsible for this. Zhuan Yu was long ago appointed by the Former King (the Zhou Emperor) to preside over the sacrifices to Mount Dongmeng. Moreover, it lies within the boundaries of our state of Lu, and the people of Zhuan Yu are natives of our state. How can such an attack be justified?"

Ran You said, "The head of the Ji Family desires it. Neither of us two wants it."

The Master (Confucius) said, "Ran You, among the sayings of Zhou Ren (an ancient sage) there is one which runs 'He who can bring his power into play steps into the ranks; he who cannot, stays behind.' Of what use are assistants such as you, who see your master in danger, but do not give him a hand; see him falling, but do not prop him up? Moreover, your plea is a false one, for if a tiger or wild buffalo escapes from its cage, or a precious ornament of tortoise-shell or jade gets broken in its box, whose fault is it?"

Ran You said, "But now Zhuan Yu is strongly fortified and is close to the fief of Fei, an important town of the Ji Family. If it is not attacked today, in days to come it will certainly be a source of disaster for our descendants."

9 周任：周朝有名的史官。

10 陈力：发挥、尽量施展自己的才力。就列：走上当官的行列，担任职务。

11 相：辅佐，帮助。古代扶引盲人的人叫“相”。引申为助手。

12 兕（sì）：古代犀牛类的野兽。或说即雌犀牛。柙（xiá）：关猛兽的木笼子。

13 椟（dú）：木制的柜子，匣子。

14 费（bì）：季氏的采邑。在今山东省费县西南，有费城。颛臾与费邑相距仅七十里，故说“近于费”。

15 疾：厌恶，痛恨。辞：托辞，借口。

16 “不患贫”句：原为“不患寡而患不均，不患贫而患不安”，清代俞樾《群经平议》以为“寡”当作“贫”，“贫”当作“寡”。《春秋繁露·度制》和《魏书·张普惠传》引此文，都是“不患贫而患不均，不患寡而患不安”。据改。朱熹说：“均，谓各得其分；安，谓上下相安。”

17 来：通“徕”。招徕，吸引，使其感化归服。

18 分崩离析：“崩”，倒塌。“析”，公开。形容集团、国家等分裂瓦解，不可收拾。当时鲁国不统一，四分五　裂，被季孙、孟孙、叔孙三大贵族所分割。

19 萧墙之内：“萧墙”，宫殿当门的小墙，或称“屏”。古代臣子进见国君，至屏而肃然起敬，

The Master (Confucius) said, "Ran You! A gentleman dislikes those who desire something but always find a pretext. For my part, I have heard the saying that the head of a state or the head of a family is not concerned about population, but about improper apportionment; he is not concerned about numbers, but about instability. For, if there is apportionment, there is no poverty. When there is harmony, there will be no lack of men. When stability reigns, there will be no danger of collapse. But when, under such circumstances as described, the people of far-off lands still do not submit, he attracted them through rites and benevolence. Once they have been attracted, he gives them security. Today you (Zhong You and Ran You)are Ji sun's ministers. The people of far-lands do not submit to him, and he is not able to attract them. Our state is tumbling and splitting up, but he can do nothing to save it and now he is planning to have a civil war within the borders of his own land. I am afraid that the troubles of Ji Sun are due not to Zhuan Yu, but to his own court."

16.2

孔子曰："天下有道，则礼乐征伐自天子出；天下无道，则礼乐征伐自诸侯出。自诸侯出，盖十世希不失矣[1]；自大夫出，五世希不失矣；陪臣执国命[2]，三世希不失矣。天下有道，则政不在大夫。天下有道，则庶人不议。"

【中译文】

孔子说："天下太平，制礼作乐，军事征伐，由天子来决定；天下无道，制礼作乐，军事征伐，由诸侯来决定。由诸侯来决定，大概传十代就很少有不衰亡的；由大夫来决定，传五代就很少有不衰亡的；由卿、大夫的家臣来掌握国家的命运，传上三代就很少有不衰亡的。天下有道，国家政权不会落在大夫手里。天下有道，老百姓就不议论朝政了。"

【注释】

1 "十世"句："世"，代。"十世"，即十代。朱熹说："先王之制，诸侯不得变礼乐，专征伐。""逆理愈甚，则其失之愈速。"因为天下无道，天子无实权，才会形成"礼乐征伐自诸侯出"的局面；再混乱，就会到"自大夫出"、"陪臣执国命"的地步。这样的政权当然不会巩固。"十世"及后面的"五世"、"三世"均为约数，只是说明逆理愈甚，则失之愈速。这也是孔子对当时各国政权变动实况进行观察研究而得出的结论。希：同"稀"。少有。

2 陪臣：卿、大夫的家臣。

【英译文】

The Master (Confucius) said, "When the right way prevails under Heaven, all orders concerning rites, music and punitive expeditions are issued by the king. Otherwise, such orders are issued by the feudal princes; and when this happens, the dynasty will rarely last ten generations. If such orders are issued by state ministers, the dynasty will rarely last five generations. If the retainers of big families seize a state's power, the dynasty will rarely last three generations. When the right way prevails under Heaven, state power will not be in the hands of state ministers and ordinary men do not talk about public affairs."

16.3

孔子曰："禄之去公室五世矣[1]，政逮于大夫四世矣[2]，故夫三桓之子孙微矣[3]。"

【中译文】

孔子说："鲁国的国君失去国家政权有五代了，政权落在大夫手里有四代了，所以，鲁国国君的子孙已衰微了。"

【注释】

1 禄：爵禄。这里代指国家政权。公室：指鲁国朝廷。五世：五代。公元前608年，鲁文公死，大夫东门遂（襄仲）杀嫡长子子赤而立宣公，掌握了鲁国政权。宣公死，政权实际上落在季氏手中。到孔子说这段话时，已又经鲁成公、鲁襄公、鲁昭公，到鲁定公，共五代。

2 逮：及，到。四世：公元前591年，鲁宣公死，季文子驱逐了东门氏，此后，由季氏为正卿，掌握了鲁国政权。从文子，经武子、平子、桓子，到孔子说这段话时，正为四代。

3 三桓：即鲁国的"三卿"：季孙氏，叔孙氏，孟孙（即仲孙）氏。因这三家都是鲁桓公的后代，故称"三桓"。这三家一直掌握鲁国政权，到鲁定公时，曾出现"陪臣执国命"的局面，三桓势力一度衰弱。

【英译文】

The Master (Confucius) said, Power over the exchequer was lost by the Duke Wen of Lu five generations ago, and government has been in the hands of Ministers for four generations. Small wonder that the descendants of the Duke Huan of Lu are fast losing their power!

16.4

孔子曰："益者三友，损者三友。友直，友谅[1]，友多闻，益矣。友便辟[2]，友善柔[3]，友便佞[4]，损矣。"

【中译文】

孔子说："有益的朋友有三种，有害的朋友也有三种。朋友刚直，朋友诚信，朋友学识广博，是有益的。朋友诡异，朋友谄媚，朋友花言巧语，是有害的。"

【注释】

1 谅：诚实。

2 便辟（piánpì）：习于摆架子装样子，内心却邪恶不正。

3 善柔：善于阿谀奉承，内心却无诚信。

4 便佞（piánnìng）：善于花言巧语，而言不符实。

【英译文】

The Master (Confucius) said, There are three sorts of friend that are profitable, and three sorts that are harmful. Friendship with the upright, with the

true-to-death and with those who have heard much is profitable. Friendship with the obsequious, friendship with those who are good at accommodating their principles, friendship with those who are clever at talk is harmful.

16.5

孔子曰："益者三乐，损者三乐。乐节礼乐，乐道人之善，乐多贤友，益矣。乐骄乐，乐佚游[1]，乐宴乐，损矣。"

【中译文】

孔子说："有益的快乐有三种，有损的快乐也有三种。以得到礼乐的调节为快乐，以赞扬别人的优点为快乐，以多交贤德的友人为快乐，是有益的。以骄奢放肆为快乐，以闲佚游荡为快乐，以宴饮纵欲为快乐，是有害的。"

【注释】

1 佚：同"逸"。安闲，休息。

【英译文】

The Master (Confucius) said, There are three sorts of pleasure that are profitable, and three sorts of pleasure that are harmful. The pleasure got from the due ordering of ritual and music, the pleasure got from discussing the good points in the conduct of others, the pleasure of having many wise friends is profitable. But pleasure got from profligate enjoyments, pleasure got from idle gadding about pleasure got from comfort and ease is harmful.

16.6

孔子曰："侍于君子有三愆[1]：言未及之而言谓之躁，言及之而不言谓之隐[2]，未见颜色而言谓之瞽[3]。"

【中译文】

孔子说："侍奉君子容易有三种过失：还未到说的时候说，叫作急躁；到该说时不说，叫作隐瞒；不看别人脸色而贸然就说，叫作盲目。"

【注释】

1 愆（qiān）：过失，差错，失误。

2 隐：隐瞒，有意缄默。

3 瞽（gǔ）：双目失明，盲人。这里比喻不能察言观色，说话不看时机就如盲人一样。

【英译文】

The Master (Confucius) said, There are three mistakes that are liable to be made when waiting upon a gentleman. Speaking before being called upon to do so; this is called forwardness. Failing to reply when called upon to do so; this is called secretiveness. To speak without first noting the expression of his face; this is called 'blindness'.

16.7

孔子曰："君子有三戒：少之时，血气未定[1]，

戒之在色；及其壮也，血气方刚，戒之在斗；及其老也，血气既衰，戒之在得[2]。”

【中译文】

孔子说：“君子有三戒：年轻时，血气还不成熟，要戒贪恋女色；到了壮年时，血气正旺盛，要戒争强好斗；到了老年时，血气已经衰弱，要戒贪得无厌。”

【注释】

1 未定：未成熟，未固定。

2 得：泛指对于名誉、地位、钱财、女色等等的贪欲、贪求。

【英译文】

The Master (Confucius) said, There are three things against which a gentleman is on his guard. In his youth, before his blood and vital humours have settled down, he is on his guard against lust. Having reached his prime, when the blood and vital humours have finally hardened, he is on his guard against strife. Having reached old age, When the blood and vital humours are already decaying, he is on his guard against avarice.

16.8

子曰：“君子有三畏[1]：畏天命，畏大人[2]，畏圣人之言。小人不知天命而不畏也，狎大人[3]，侮圣人之言。”

【中译文】

孔子说：“君子有三种敬畏：敬畏天命，敬畏在高位的人，敬畏圣人的话。小人不知天命而不敬畏，不尊重在上位的人，蔑视圣人的话。”

【注释】

1 畏：怕。这里指心存敬畏，敬服。要时时处处注意修身诫己，有敬慎之心。

2 大人：在高位的贵族、官僚。

3 狎（xiá）：狎侮，轻慢，不尊重。

【英译文】

The Master (Confucius) said, There are three things that a gentleman fears: he fears the will of Heaven, he fears great men, he fears the words of the Divine Sages. The petty man does not know the will of Heaven and so does not fear it. He treats great men with contempt, and scoffs at the words of the Divine Sages.

16.9

孔子曰：“生而知之者，上也；学而知之者，次也；困而学之，又其次也；困而不学，民斯为下矣。”

【中译文】

孔子说：“天赋高、不学而知，是上等；经过学习

而获得知识，是次一等；遇到困难然后学习，是再次一等；遇到困难还不学习，这样的人就是下等了。”

【英译文】

The Master (Confucius) said, Highest are those who are born wise. Next are those who become wise by learning. After them come those who have to toil painfully in order to acquire learning. Finally, to the lowest class of the common people belong those who toil painfully without ever managing to learn.

16.10

孔子曰：“君子有九思：视思明，听思聪，色思温，貌思恭，言思忠，事思敬，疑思问，忿思难[1]，见得思义。”

【中译文】

孔子说：“君子有九种考虑：看，考虑是否看得清楚；听，考虑是否听得明白；脸色，考虑是否温和；态度，考虑是否庄重恭敬；说话，考虑是否忠诚老实；做事，考虑是否认真谨慎；有疑难，考虑应该询问请教别人；发火发怒，考虑是否会产生后患；见到财利，考虑是否合于仁义。”

【注释】

1 难（nàn）：这里指发怒可能带来的灾难、留下的后患。

【英译文】

The Master (Confucius) said, The gentleman has nine cares. In seeing he is careful to see clearly, in hearing he is careful to hear distinctly, in his looks he is careful to be kindly; in his manner to be respectful, in his words to be loyal, in his work to be diligent. When in doubt he is careful to ask for information; when angry he has a care for the consequences, and when he sees a chance of gain, he thinks carefully whether the pursuit of it would be consonant with the Right.

16.11

孔子曰：“见善如不及，见不善如探汤[1]。吾见其人矣，吾闻其语矣。隐居以求其志，行义以达其道[2]。吾闻其语矣，未见其人也。”

【中译文】

孔子说：“看见善的就努力学习，如同怕自己赶不上似的；看见邪恶，如同把手伸进开水要赶快避开。我见过这种人，我听过这种话。以隐居来求得保全自己的志向，以实行仁义来贯彻自己的主张。我听过这种话，没见过这种人。”

【注释】

1 探汤：“汤”，开水，热水。把手伸到滚烫的水里。指要赶紧躲避开。

2 达：达到，全面贯彻。

【英译文】

The Master (Confucius)said, "When seeing what is good, pursue it as though you could never quite come to it; when seeing what is not good, elude it as though you dared not put your fingers into boiling water. I have heard this saying and I have seen such men. I have heard of men living in seclusion in order to preserve their integrity and doing what is right to achieve their way of life. But I have never seen such men."

16.12

齐景公有马千驷[1]，死之日，民无德而称焉。伯夷、叔齐饿于首阳之下[2]，民到于今称之。（诚不以富，亦只以异。）[3] 其斯之谓与。

【中译文】

齐景公有四千匹马，死的时候，老百姓认为他没有美德可称颂。伯夷、叔齐饿死在首阳山下，但老百姓到现在还称颂他们。“这实在不是因为富有，而是因为品德优秀。”说的就是这个意思吧。

【注释】

1 千驷：古代一辆车套四匹马，驷就是四匹马的统称。千驷就是四千匹马。作为诸侯而有马千驷，在当时是豪侈而越制的。

2 首阳：首阳山。又称雷首山，独领山。在今山西省运城（一说永济）县南，为当年伯夷、叔齐采薇隐居处。南山有古冢，松柏茂盛，传说即伯夷、叔齐的墓。关于伯夷、叔齐，已见前《公冶长篇第五》第二十三章注，可参阅。

3 “诚不”句：这两句原在《颜渊篇第十二》第十　章中。有人说应加在这里，与后句“其斯之谓与”衔接。姑按前人之说，加括号补入。注详见《颜渊篇第十二》。

【英译文】

Duke Jing of Qi had a thousand teams of horses, but on the day he died the people could think of no good deed for which to praise him. Bo Yi and Shu Qi died of hunger at the foot of Mount Shouyang, and the people praise them to the present day. Isn't this meaningful?

16.13

陈亢问于伯鱼曰[1]：“子亦有异闻乎？”

对曰：“未也。尝独立，鲤趋而过庭[2]。曰：‘学《诗》乎？’对曰：‘未也’。‘不学《诗》无以言。’鲤退而学《诗》。他日，又独立，鲤趋而过庭。曰：‘学礼乎？’对曰：‘未也。’‘不学礼，无以立。’鲤退而学礼。闻斯二者。”

陈亢退而喜曰：“问一得三，闻《诗》，闻礼，又闻君子之远其子也[3]。”

【中译文】

陈亢问伯鱼："您从老师那里得到过什么特别的教导吗？"伯鱼回答："没有。一次他一个人站在那里，我轻步经过庭院。他问：'学过《诗经》吗？'我回答：'没有。'他说'不学《诗经》，在社会交往中就不会说话。'我回去就学《诗经》。又一次，他又一个人站在那里，我轻步经过庭院。他问：'学过礼吗？'我回答：'没有。'他说：'不学礼，在社会上做人做事不能立足。'我回去就学礼。我只听说过这两件事。"亢回去高兴地说："问了一件事，得到三个收获：听学《诗经》的意义，听到学礼的好处，又听到君子不偏爱自己的儿子。"

【注释】

1 陈亢：字子禽。参阅《学而篇第一》第十章注。鱼：孔子的儿子，名鲤，字伯鱼。

2 趋：小步快速而行，以示恭敬。

3 远：远离，避开，不亲近。这里指对自己的儿子不向，没有偏爱，没有特殊照顾和过分关照

【英译文】

Chen Kang asked Bo Yu (the son of Confucius), "Have you ever received any different teaching from your father?"

He replied, "No. But once when I was passing hurriedly through the courtyard, I met my father standing alone, and he said, 'Have you studied The Book of Poetry?' I replied, 'Not yet.' He said, 'If you do not study The Book of Poetry, you won't be able to carry on a conversation.' Thereupon I withdrew and studied The Book of Poetry. Another day I met him standing alone as I passed through the courtyard and he said, 'Have you studied The Book of Rites?' I replied, 'Not yet.' He said, 'If you do not study The Book of Rites, you will never take your stand!' So I withdrew and studied The Book of Rites. These are the two pieces of instruction I have received from my father."

Chen Kang went away rejoicing and said, "I asked about one thing and have learned three-something about The Book of Poetry, something about The Book of Rites, and also that a true gentleman has no prejudice in favor of his son."

16. 14

邦君之妻[1]，君称之曰夫人，夫人自称曰童[2]；邦人称之曰君夫人，称诸异邦曰寡小君[3]；邦人称之亦曰君夫人。

【中译文】

国君的妻子，国君称她为"夫人"，她自称"小童"；国内的人称她为"君夫人"，在其他国家人面前称她为"寡小君"；其他国家的人也称她"君夫人"。

【注释】

1 邦君：指诸侯国的国君。

2 小童：谦称。犹说自己无知如童子。

3 诸："之于"的合音。

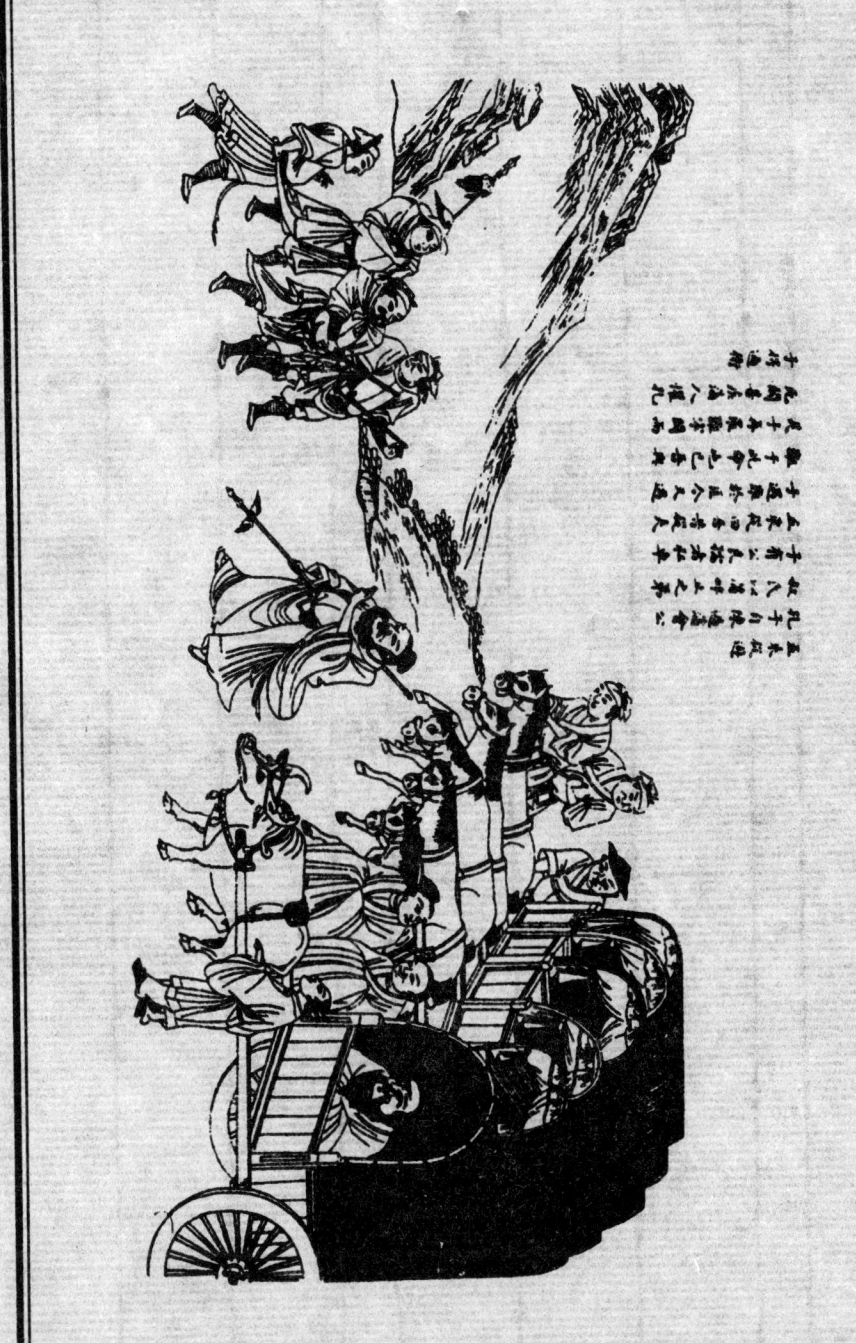

Five Coaches Travelling Along with Confucius

【英译文】

The wife of a prince is called Lady by her husband. She calls herself child. The people call her the Prince's Lady. When she is mentioned to officials of another state she is called Our Princess. But the people of another state likewise call her the Prince's Lady.

阳货篇第十七（共二十六章）

On Governing the State According to Ritural

17.1

阳货欲见孔子[1]，孔子不见，归孔子豚[2]。

孔子时其亡也[3]，而往拜之。

遇诸涂[4]。

谓孔子曰："来！予与尔言。"曰："怀其宝而迷其邦[5]，可谓仁乎？"曰："不可。""好从事而亟失时[6]，可谓知乎[7]？"曰："不可。""日月逝矣，岁不我与[8]。"

孔子曰："诺，吾将仕矣。"

【中译文】

阳货想拜见孔子，孔子不见，他便赠送给孔子一只蒸熟的小猪。孔子趁阳货不在家时回拜他。两人却在途中遇见了。阳货对孔子说："过来！我有话对你说。"随后说："把自己的宝物藏在怀里，听任国家迷乱，这样做可以称为仁吗？"孔子说："不可以。"阳货又说："喜欢参与政事而又屡次错过机会，可以称为智吗？"孔子说："不可以。"阳货又说："时间消逝了，岁月是不等待人的。"孔子说："好吧，我将要去做官了。"

【注释】

1 阳货：又名阳虎，杨虎。鲁国季氏的家臣。曾一度掌握了季氏一家的大权，甚而掌握了鲁国的大权，是孔子所讥的"陪臣执国命"的人物。阳货为了发展自己的势力，极力拉孔子给他做事。但孔子不愿随附于阳货，故采取设法避回的态度。后阳货因企图消除三桓未成而逃往国外，孔子最终也未仕于阳货。

2 归：同"馈"。赠送。豚（tún）：小猪。这里指熟了的小猪。按照当时的礼节，地位高的人赠送礼物给地位低的人，受赠者如果不在家，没能当面接受，事后应当回拜，因为孔子一直不愿见阳货，阳货就用这种办法，想以礼节逼迫孔子去回拜。

3 时：同"伺"。意指窥伺，暗中打听，探听消息。亡：同"无"。这里指不在家。

4 涂：同"途"。途中，半道上。

5 迷其邦：听任国家迷乱，政局动荡不安。

6 亟（qì）：副词。屡次。

7 知：同"智"。

8 岁不我与：即"岁不与我"，年岁不等待我。"与"指一起。这里有等待之意。

【英译文】

Yang Huo wanted to see the Master; but the Master would not see him. He sent the Master a sucking pig. The Master, choosing a time when he knew Yang Huo would not be at home, went to tender acknowledgment; but met him

in the road. He spoke to the Master, saying, Come here, I have something to say to you. What he said was, Can one who hides his jewel in his bosom and lets his country continue to go astray be called Good? Certainly not. Can one who longs to take part in affairs, yet time after time misses the opportunity to do so-can such a one be called wise? Certainly not. The days and months go by, the years do not wait upon our bidding. The Master said, All right; I am going to accept public office.

17.2

子曰："性相近也[1]，习相远也[2]。"

【中译文】

孔子说："人的本性是相近的，由于环境不同积习日异，才相距甚远了。"

【注释】

1 性：人的本性，性情，先天的智力、气质。

2 习相远：指由于社会影响，所受教育不同，习俗气的沾染有别，人的后天的行为习惯会有很大差异。这是勉励人为学，通过学习提高自己的修养。

【英译文】

The Master (Confucius) said, By nature, near together, by practice far apart.

17.3

子曰："唯上知与下愚不移[1]。"

【中译文】

孔子说："只有上等聪明的人和下等愚笨的人是无法改变的。"

【注释】

1 知：同"智"。不移：不可移易、改变。

【英译文】

The Master (Confucius) said, It is only the very wisest and the very stupidest who cannot change.

17.4

子之武城[1]，闻弦歌之声。夫子莞尔而笑[2]，曰："割鸡焉用牛刀？"子游对曰："昔者偃也闻诸夫子曰[3]：'君子学道则爱人，小人学道则易使也。'"子曰："二三子，偃之言是也。前言戏之耳[4]。"

【中译文】

孔子到了武城，听见弹琴唱歌的声音。孔子微笑着说："杀鸡何必用牛刀呢？"子游回答说："过去我听老师说：'君子学道就能惠爱百姓；一般老百姓学了

道，就容易役使了。’”孔子对随从的弟子说：“诸位，言偃说的是对的。我刚才说的话不过是开玩笑罢了。”

【注释】

1 武城：鲁国的一个小城邑。在今山东省嘉祥县境。一说，指南武城，在今山东省费县西南。公元前554年，鲁襄公筑武城以御齐。另说，即城武县，在今山东省菏泽市西北七十里，有弦歌里。当时，言偃（子游）任武城行政长官。

2 莞（wǎn）尔：微笑的样子。

3 诸：“之于”的合音。

4 戏：开玩笑，逗趣。

【英译文】

When the Master went to Wu Cheng, he heard the sound of stringed instruments and singing. Our Master said with a gentle smile, 'To kill a chicken one does not use an ox-cleaver.' Zi You replied, I remember once hearing you say, 'A gentleman who has studied the Way will be all the tenderer towards his fellow-men; a commoner who has studied the Way will be all the easier to employ.' The Master said, My disciples, what he says is quite true. What I said just now was only meant as a joke.

17.5

公山弗扰以费畔[1]，召，子欲往。子路不说，曰：“末之也已[2]，何必公山氏之之也[3]？”子曰：

“夫召我者，而岂徒哉？如有用我者，吾其为东周乎[4]！”

【中译文】

公山弗扰据费邑叛乱，召见孔子，孔子想去。子路很不高兴，说：“没有可去的地方就算了，何必非去公山氏那里呢？”孔子说：“召我去的人，难道会让我白去吗？如果有人用我，我就要在东方复兴周王朝的繁荣了。”

【注释】

1 公山费扰：疑即《左传》定公五年、八年、十二年及哀公八年提到的公山不狃（niǔ）。季氏家臣，后据费邑叛季氏，失败后逃亡齐国，又奔吴。畔：同“叛”。

2 末之也已：没有可去的地方就算了。“末”，没有。“之”，去，往。“已”，止，算了。

3 “何必”句：何必非去公山氏那个地方呢？句中第一个“之”是助词，起把宾语提前的语法作用。第二个“之”是动词，去，往。

4 “吾其”句：孔子此句意为：将要在东方建立起一个西周式的社会，使文王武王之道重现于东方。关于此章所说孔子拟应公山弗扰之召事，许多学者提出质疑一、《左传·定公十二年》记公山不狃叛鲁之事，并无召请孔子的记载，且当时孔子正任鲁国司寇，还派兵打败了公山不狃。二、依本章所记，孔子显有“助

叛"之嫌，这与孔子的一贯主张不符。史实究竟如何，已不可确考。

【英译文】

When Gong Shan Fu rao held the fief of Fei in revolt, he sent for the Master, who would have liked to go; but Zi Lu did not approve of this and said to the Master, After having refused in so many cases, why go to Kung-shan of all people? The Master said, It cannot be for nothing that he has sent for me. If anyone were to use me, I believe I could make a 'Chou in the east'.

17.6

子张问仁于孔子。孔子曰："能行五者于天下为仁矣。""请问之。"曰："恭，宽，信，敏，惠。恭则不侮，宽则得众，信则人任焉，敏则有功，惠则足以使人。"

【中译文】

子张向孔子问怎样做到仁，孔子说："能在天下实行这五项，就做到了仁。"子张说："请问哪五项？"孔子说："恭敬，宽厚，守信，勤敏，慈惠。恭敬庄重，就不会受到侮慢；宽厚，就能获得众人拥护；守信，就能得到别人的任用；勤敏，就能取得成功；慈惠，就完全能更好地指挥别人。"

【英译文】

Zi Zhang asked the Master about Goodness. The Master said, He who could put the Five into practice everywhere under Heaven would be Good. Zi Zhang begged to hear what these were. The Master said, Courtesy, breadth, good faith, diligence and clemency. 'He who is courteous is not scorned, he who is broad wins the multitude, he who is of good faith is trusted by the people, he who is diligent succeeds in all he undertakes, he who is clement can get service from the people.

17.7

佛肸召[1]，子欲往。子路曰："昔者由也闻诸夫子曰：'亲于其身为不善者，君子不入也。'佛肸以中牟畔[2]，子之往也，如之何？"子曰："然，有是言也。不曰坚乎，磨而不磷[3]？不曰白乎，涅而不缁[4]？吾岂匏瓜也哉[5]？焉能系而不食？"

【中译文】

佛肸召请，孔子想去。子路说："从前我听老师说过：'直接做坏事的人那里，君子是不去的。'佛肸据中牟叛乱，您要去，为什么？"孔子说："是的，我说过这话。但不是说坚硬的东西，磨也磨不薄吗？不是说洁白的东西，染也染不黑吗？我难道像匏瓜吗？怎能只挂着不吃呢？"

【注释】

1 佛肸（bì xī）：晋国大夫范中行的家臣，是中牟城的行政长官。公元前490年，晋国赵简子攻打范氏，包围中牟，佛肸抵抗。佛肸召请孔子，就在这时（事见《左传·哀公五年》）。

2 中牟：晋国地名，约在今河北省邢台市和邯郸市之间。一说，在今河南省鹤壁市西，古代牟山之侧。畔同“叛”。

3 磷（lìn）：本义是薄石。引申为把石头磨薄，使其受到磨损。

4 涅（niè）：一种矿物，也叫“皂矾”，古代用作黑色染料。这里用作动词，染黑。缁（zī）：黑色。

5 匏（páo）瓜：葫芦的一种，果实比一般葫芦大。老后中空轻于水，可系于腰助人渡河泅水；或可对半剖开，做水瓢舀水用。

【英译文】

Bi Xi summoned the Master, and he would have liked to go. But Zi Lu said, I remember your once saying, 'Into the house of one who is in his own person doing what is evil, the gentleman will not enter.' Bi Xi is holding Zhongmu in revolt. How can you think of going to him? The Master said, It is true that there is such a saying. But is it not also said that there are things 'So hard that no grinding will ever wear them down', that there are things 'So white that no steeping will ever make them black'? Am I indeed to be forever like the bitter gourd that is only fit to hang up, but not to eat?

17.8

子曰：“由也，女闻六言六蔽矣乎[1]？”对曰：“未也。”“居[2]！吾语女。好仁不好学，其蔽也愚；好知不好学[3]，其蔽也荡[4]；好信不好学，其蔽也贼[5]；好直不好学，其蔽也绞[6]；好勇不好学，其蔽也乱；好刚不好学，其蔽也狂。”

【中译文】

孔子说：“仲由，你听说过六种美德和六种弊病吗？”子路回答：“没有。”孔子说：“坐下来！我告诉你。爱好仁德却不好学习，其弊病是易受人愚弄；爱好聪明却不好学习，其弊病是放荡不羁；爱好诚实却不好学习，其弊病是易被人利用，反害了自己；直率却不好学习，其弊病是说话尖刻刺人；爱好勇敢却不好学习，其弊病是容易闹乱子闯祸；爱好刚强却不好学习，其弊病是狂妄自大。”

【注释】

1 女：同“汝”。你。六言：六个字，即文中的仁、知、信、直、勇、刚等德行的六个方面。蔽：通“弊”。弊病，害处。

2 居：坐。

3 知：同“智”。

4 荡：放荡不羁。

5 贼：害，伤害。这里指容易给自己带来伤害。
6 绞：说话尖酸刻薄，不通情理。

【英译文】

The Master (Confucius) said, Zhong You, have you ever been told of the Six Sayings about the Six Degenerations? Zi Lu replied, No, never. The Master said, Come, then; I will tell you. Love of Goodness without love of learning degenerates into silliness. Love of wisdom without love of learning degenerates into utter lack of principle. Love of keeping promises without love of learning degenerates into villainy. Love of uprightness without love of learning degenerates into harshness. Love of courage without love of learning degenerates into turbulence. Love of courage without love of learning degenerates into mere recklessness.

17.9

子曰："小子何莫学夫《诗》？《诗》可以兴[1]，可以观[2]，可以群[3]，可以怨[4]；迩之事父[5]，远之事君；多识于鸟兽草木之名。"

【中译文】

孔子说："弟子们怎么不学习《诗经》呢？《诗经》可以联想，可以观察，可以使人合群，可以表达讽喻；近可以侍奉父母，远可以事奉君主；还可以认识鸟兽草木的名称。"

【英译文】

The Master (Confucius) said, Little ones, Why is it that none of you study the Book of Poetry? For it it will help you to incite people's emotions, to observe their feelings, to keep company, to express your grievances. They may be used at home in the service of one's father, abroad, in the service of one's prince. Moreover, they will widen your acquaintance with the names of birds, beasts, plants and trees.

17.10

子谓伯鱼曰："女为《周南》《召南》矣乎[1]？人而不为《周南》《召南》，其犹正墙面而立也与[2]！"

【中译文】

孔子对伯鱼说："你学了《周南》《召南》了吗？人如果不学《周南》《召南》，就好像面对墙壁站着啊！"

【注释】

1 为：本义是做。这里指学习。周南，召（shào）南：《诗经》十五国风中的第一、第二两部分。本为地名，"周南"约在汉水流域东部，今陕西、河南之间直到湖北。"召南"约在汉水流域西部，今河南、湖北之间。这两个地域收集在《诗经》中的民歌，就叫《周南》《召南》。孔子认为《周南》《召南》中有许多修养齐家的道理，故提倡学习，并加以重视。

2 “其犹”句：“正”，对着。就好像面对着墙壁站着比喻被阻挡而无法向前，一物无所见，一步不可行。一说《周南》《召南》中的诗，多用于乡乐，是众人合唱的，不用来独诵。如果一个人不会《周南》《召南》，那就得独自保持沉默虽在合唱的人群之中，也像面对着墙壁而孤立一般。

【英译文】

The Master (Confucius) said to Bo Yu, Have you done the Chou Nan and the Shao Nan (the first two sections of the Book of poetry) yet? He who has not even done the Chou Nan and the Shao Nan is as though he stood with his face pressed against a wall!

17.11

子曰：“礼云礼云，玉帛云乎哉[1]！乐云乐云，钟鼓云乎哉[2]？”

【中译文】

孔子说：“礼呀礼呀，只是指玉帛之类的礼器吗？乐呀乐呀，只是指钟鼓之类的乐器吗？”

【注释】

1 玉帛：指古代举行礼仪时使用的玉器、丝帛等礼器、礼品。

2 钟鼓：古代乐器。朱熹说：“敬而将之以玉帛，则为礼；和而发之以钟鼓，则为乐。”这说明礼乐之可贵在于在百姓中提倡“敬”、“和”。如果只是在形式上摆玉帛、敲钟鼓，而忽略了它的深刻的内容，那就失去了礼乐本来的意义与作用。

【英译文】

The Master (Confucius) said, Ritual, ritual! Does it mean no more than presents of jade and silk? Music, music! Does it mean no more than bells and drums?

17.12

子曰：“色厉而内荏[1]，譬诸小人，其犹穿窬之盗也与[2]！”

【中译文】

孔子说：“外表神色严厉而内心怯弱，以小人来作比喻，就像是挖墙穿洞的小偷吧！”

【注释】

1 色厉内荏：外貌似乎刚强威严，而内心却柔弱怯惧。“色”，神色，脸色，外表的样子。“荏（rěn）”，软弱，怯懦，虚弱。

2 穿：挖，透，破。窬（yú）：洞，窟窿。从墙上爬过去也叫窬。

【英译文】

The Master (Confucius) said, To assume an outward air of fierceness when inwardly trembling is (to take a comparison from low walks of life) as dishonest as to sneak into places where one has no right to be, by boring a hole or climbing through a gap.

17.13

子曰："乡愿[1]，德之贼也[2]。"

【中译文】

孔子说："所谓不分是非的好好先生，是败坏道德的人。"

【注释】

1 乡愿：特指当时社会上那种不分是非，同于流俗，言行不一，伪善欺世，处处讨好，谁也不得罪的乡里中以"谨厚老实"为人称道的"老好人"。孔子尖锐地指出：这种"乡愿"，言行不符，实际上是似德非德而乱乎德的人，乃德之"贼"。世人对之不可不辨。而后，孟子更清楚地说明这种人乃是"同乎流俗，合乎污世"的人。虽然表面上看，是个对乡人全不得罪的"好好先生"，其实，他抹煞了是非，混淆了善恶，不主持正义，不抵制坏人坏事，全然成为危害道德的人（见《孟子·尽心下》）。"愿"，谨厚，老实。

2 贼：败坏，侵害，危害。

【英译文】

The Master (Confucius) said, The 'honest villager' spoils true virtue.

17.14

子曰："道听而涂说[1]，德之弃也。"

【中译文】

孔子说："在路上听到什么就四处传播，是道德所唾弃的。"

【注释】

1 "道听"句：在道上听到的不可靠的传闻，途中又向别人传说。"涂"，同"途"。

【英译文】

The Master (Confucius) said, To tell in the lane what you have heard on the way is to abandon your virtue.

17.15

子曰："鄙夫可与事君也与哉[1]？其未得之也，患得之[2]。既得之，患失之。苟患失之，无所不至矣[3]。"

【中译文】

孔子说："粗鄙之人怎么可以一起侍奉君主呢？他

没得到时，总担心得不到。既得到了，又担心失掉。假如老担心失掉，那就无论什么事都做得出来了。”

【注释】

1 鄙夫：鄙陋、庸俗、道德品质恶劣的人。

2 患得之：实际上是“患不能得之”的意思。“患”，怕，担心。

3 无所不至：无所不用其极，无所不为。

【英译文】

The Master (Confucius) said, How could one ever possibly serve one's prince alongside of such low-down creatures? Before they have got office, they think about nothing but how to get it; and when they have got it, all they care about is to avoid losing it. And so soon as they see themselves in the slightest danger of losing it, there is no length to which they will not go.

17.16

子曰：“古者民有三疾[1]，今也或是之亡也[2]。古之狂也肆，今之狂也荡；古之矜也廉[3]，今之矜也忿戾[4]；古之愚也直，今之愚也诈而已矣。”

【中译文】

孔子说：“古代的百姓有三种毛病，今人连这些毛病也比不上古人了。古代轻狂的人不过放肆直言，不拘小节，现在轻狂的人却是放荡越礼，毫无顾忌；古代骄傲的人不过是持守过严，不可触犯，现在骄傲的人却是忿怨乖戾，蛮横无理；古代愚笨的人不过简单直率，现在愚笨的人却是虚伪欺诈自以为聪明罢了。”

【注释】

1 疾：本义是病。这里指气质上的缺点。由于世风日下，今人的缺点毛病也无法同古人的缺点毛病相比了。古人气质上有缺点的尚且朴实可贵，今人则变得更加道德低下，风俗日衰了。

2 亡：同“无”。

3 矜（jīn）：骄傲，自尊自大。廉：本义是器物的棱角。这里引申为不可触犯，碰不得，惹不得。

4 忿戾（lì）：凶恶好争，蛮横无理。

【英译文】

The Master (Confucius) said, In old days the common people had three faults, part of which they have now lost. In old days the impetuous were merely impatient of small restraints; now they are utterly insubordinate. In old days the proud were stiff and formal; now they are touchy and quarrelsome. In old days simpletons were at any rate straightforward; but now 'simple-mindedness' exists only as a device of the impostor.

17.17

子曰：“巧言令色，鲜矣仁[1]。”

【中译文】

孔子说：“花言巧语，故作和悦之色，这种人是很

少有仁德的。”

【注释】

1 本章与《学而篇第一》第三章重复。可参阅。

【英译文】

The Master (Confucius) said, Clever talk and a pretentious manner have little to do with virtue.

17.18

子曰：“恶紫之夺朱也[1]，恶郑声之乱雅乐也，恶利口之覆邦家者。”

【中译文】

孔子说：“厌恶紫色比红色抢眼，厌恶郑国的音乐扰乱雅乐，厌恶以巧言善辩的嘴巴来败亡国家的人。”

【注释】

1 恶（wù）：厌恶，讨厌。紫之夺朱：“夺”，强行取得，取代，顶替。“朱”，大红色。古代传统称为正色。紫是红色和蓝色混合而成的颜色，虽与红色接近，然而不是正色而是杂色。但在春秋时期，史载鲁桓公和齐桓公都喜欢穿紫色衣服，可见那时紫色已取代了朱色的传统地位，连诸侯的衣服都以紫色为正色了。而孔子认为：朱色的光彩与地位不应被紫色所夺去。

【英译文】

The Master (Confucius) said, I hate to see roan killing red, I hate to see the tunes of Zheng State corrupting Court music, I hate to see sharp mouths overturning kingdoms and clans.

17.19

子曰：“予欲无言。”子贡曰：“子如不言，则小子何述焉？”子曰：“天何言哉？四时行焉[1]，百物生焉。天何言哉？”

【中译文】

孔子说：“我不想讲述了。”子贡说：“您如果不讲述，那么弟子们还传述什么呢？”孔子说：“天何尝讲述呢？四季照样运行不息，各种动植物照样发育生长。天何尝讲述呢？”

【注释】

1 四时：指春、夏、秋、冬四季。

【英译文】

The Master (Confucius) said, I would much rather not have to talk. Zi Gong said, If our Master did not talk, what should we little ones have to hand down about him? The Master said, Heaven does not speak; yet the four seasons run their course thereby, the hundred creatures, each after its kind, are born thereby. Heaven does no speaking!

17.20

孺悲欲见孔子[1]，孔子辞以疾。将命者出户[2]，取瑟而歌，使之闻之。

【中译文】

孺悲想见孔子，孔子推辞说有病。传话的人出了门，孔子拿过琴来弹唱，让孺悲听到。

【注释】

1 孺悲：鲁国人。鲁哀公曾派孺悲向孔子学习士丧礼。孔子这次为何不愿见孺悲，原因不明。

2 将命者：传话的人。

【英译文】

Ru Bei wanted to see the Master. The Master excused himself on the ground of ill-health. But when the man who had brought the message was going out through the door he took up his zithern and sang, talking good care that the messenger should hear.

17.21

宰我问："三年之丧，期已久矣[1]。君子三年不为礼，礼必坏；三年不为乐，乐必崩。旧谷既没，新谷既升，钻燧改火[2]，期可已矣[3]。"

子曰："食夫稻[4]，衣夫锦，于女安乎[5]？"曰："安。"

"女安，则为之！夫君子之居丧，食旨不甘[6]，闻乐不乐[7]，居处不安[8]，故不为也。今女安，则为之！"

宰我出，子曰："予之不仁也！子生三年，然后免于父母之怀。夫三年之丧，天下之通丧也。予也有三年之爱于其父母乎[9]？"

【中译文】

宰我问："三年守孝，未免太久了。君子三年不讲习礼，礼必然荒废败坏；三年不演奏音乐，音乐必然生疏忘记。旧谷子已吃完，新谷子已上场，取火用的木料也都轮了一遍，守孝一周年就可以了。"孔子说："父母去世你吃大米饭，穿锦绸缎，心安吗？"宰我说："心安。"孔子说："你心安，就这样做吧！君子居丧守孝，吃美味不觉香甜，听音乐不觉快乐，住好房子不觉安适，所以不那样做。如今你心安，就去做吧！"宰我出去后，孔子说："宰予真是不仁爱啊！孩子生下三年之后，才能脱离父母的怀抱。为父母守孝三年，是天下通行的规则。宰予难道就没得到父母三年的护爱吗？

【注释】

1 期：时间，期限。

2 钻燧改火："燧（suì）"，木燧，古代钻木取火的

工具。古人钻木取火，所用的木料四季不同。春天用榆柳，孟夏与仲夏用枣杏，季夏用桑柘，秋天用柞楢，冬天用槐檀。各种木料一年轮用一遍，第二年按上年的次序依次取用，叫“改火”。钻燧改火，即指过了一年。

3 期：指一周年。

4 食夫稻：“夫”，指示代词。这，那。古代水稻的种植面积很小，大米是很珍贵的粮食，居丧者更不宜食。因按礼“父母之丧，既殡，食粥，粗衰。既葬，疏食，水饮，受以成布期而小祥，始食菜果……。”（朱熹《四书集注》）

5 女：同“汝”。你。

6 旨：美味，好吃的食物。

7 乐：第一个“乐”，指音乐。第二个“乐”，指快乐。

8 居处：指住在平时所住的好房子里。古代守孝，应在父母坟墓附近搭一个临时性的草棚子或住茅草房，睡在地下草苫子上，以表示不忍心住在安适的屋子里。

9 “予也”句：“于”，给，与。一说，“于”，自，从。则此句意为：难道宰予没从父母那里得到过三年的爱护抚育吗？

【英译文】

Zai Wo asked about the three years' mourning saying, "Three years' mourning is too long. If a gentleman suspends his practice of rites for three years, rites

will certainly decay; if for three years he makes no music, music will certainly be destroyed. In one year the old crops have already vanished, new crops have come up, and woods for making fire finished their cycle. (Woods for making fire change every season, and the new fire is in each case kindled on the wood of a tree appropriate to the season). Surely a year's period of mourning would be enough." The Master said, "Would you then feel at ease in eating good rice and wearing silk brocades?"

Zai Wo said, "Quite at ease."

The Master (Confucius) said, "If you would really feel at ease, then do so. But when a gentleman is in mourning, if the eats dainties, he does not relish them; if he hears music, it does not please him; if he lives in his normal resting-place, he is not comfortable, Hence he abstains from these things. But if you would really feel at ease, then go and do them."

When Zai Wo had gone out, the Master said, "How inbuman Zai Wo is! Only when a child is three years old does it leave its parents' arms. Three years' mourning is the universal mourning everywhere under Heaven. And Zai Wo-was he not loved dearly by his parents for three years?"

17.22

子曰：“饱食终日[1]，无所用心，难矣哉！不有博弈者乎[2]？为之，犹贤乎已[3]。”

【中译文】

孔子说：“饱食终日，无所用心，这有些太难受了吧。不是有下棋的游戏吗？下下棋，也比什么都不干要好些。”

【注释】

1 终日：整天。

2 博：古代一种棋局游戏，用六箸十二棋为博具，以争输赢。弈（yì）：围棋。

3 贤：好，胜过，超过。已：止。指什么都不干。

【英译文】

The Master (Confucius) said, "Those who do nothing all day but cram themselves with food are no good! Are there not games such as draughts? Playing them would surely be better than doing nothing at all."

17.23

子路曰："君子尚勇乎？"子曰："君子义以为上。君子有勇而无义为乱，小人有勇而无义为盗。"

【中译文】

子路问道："君子崇尚勇敢吗？"孔子说："君子以义为最高尚。君子有勇而无义，就会犯上作乱；小人有勇而无义，就会做强盗。"

【英译文】

Zi Lu said, Is courage to be prized by a gentleman? The Master said, A gentleman gives the first place to Right. If a gentleman has courage but neglects Right, he becomes turbulent. If a petty man has courage but neglects Right, he becomes a thief.

17.24

子贡曰："君子亦有恶乎？"子曰："有恶。恶称人之恶者，恶居下流而讪上者[1]，恶勇而无礼者，恶果敢而窒者[2]。"

曰："赐也亦有恶乎？""恶徼以为知者[3]，恶不孙以为勇者[4]，恶讦以为直者[5]。"

【中译文】

子贡问道："君子也有所不容、有所憎恶吗？"孔子说："有。厌恶专讲别人坏处的人，厌恶下属诽谤上级，厌恶勇敢而不懂礼的人，厌恶固执不通事理的人。"孔子又说："子贡，你也有所厌恶吗？"子贡说："厌恶掠人之美却自以为聪明的人，厌恶不谦逊却自以为勇敢的人，厌恶揭发攻击别人却自以为直爽的人。"

【注释】

1 流：据清乾隆年间经学大家惠栋《九经古义》和清嘉庆年间学者冯登府《论语异文考证》，"流"字衍。晚唐以前的《论语》版本中无"流"字，至宋代，才有此衍误。讪（shàn）：诽谤，讥讽，诋毁。以言毁人称谤，在下谤上称讪。

2 窒（zhì）：阻塞，不通。引申为固执，头脑僵化，顽固不化。

3 徼（jiāo）：抄袭，窃取，剽窃他人的知识成果（如言论、学问、见解、做出的成绩等）。一说，私察他人之言行动静，而自作聪明，假以为知。知：同“智”。

4 孙：同“逊”。

5 讦（jié）：攻击别人的短处，揭发别人的隐私。

【英译文】

Zi Gong said, Surely even the gentleman must have his hatreds. The Master said, He has his hatreds. He hates those who point out what is hateful in others. He hates those who dwelling in low estate revile all who are above them. He hates those who love deeds of daring but neglect ritual. He hates those who are active and venturesome, but are violent in temper. I suppose you also have your hatreds? Zi Gong said, I hate those who mistake cunning for wisdom. I hat those who mistake insubordination for courage. I hate those who mistake tale-bearing for honesty.

17.25

子曰：“唯女子与小人为难养也[1]，近之则不孙[2]，远之则怨。”

【中译文】

孔子说：“唯独女婢妾和小人是难以相处的。亲近他们，就无礼；疏远他们，就怨恨。”

【注释】

1 养：供养，共同相处。这里主要指的是对婢妾，

对仆隶下人，故用“养“字。

2 不孙：指不恭顺，不守规矩，放肆无礼。“孙”，同“逊”。

【英译文】

The Master (Confucius) said, Women and petty men are very hard to deal with. If you are friendly with them, they get out of hand, and if you keep your distance, they resent it.

17.26

子曰：“年四十而见恶焉[1]，其终也已。”

【中译文】

孔子说：“年纪到了四十岁还被人厌恶，那这辈子差不多不行了。”

【注释】

1 见恶：被别人所厌恶，所讨厌。“见”，助词，表示被动。

【英译文】

The Master said, One who has reached the age of forty and is still disliked will be so till the end.

微子篇第十八（共十一章）

The Attitude Towards the World

18.1

微子去之[1]，箕子为之奴[2]，比干谏而死[3]。孔子曰：“殷有三仁焉！”

【中译文】

微子离开了纣王，箕子被纣王拘囚降为奴隶，比干屡次劝谏被纣王杀死。孔子说：“殷朝有三位仁人啊！”

【注释】

1 微子：名启，采邑在微（今山西省潞城县东北）。微子是纣王的同母兄，但微子出生时其母只是帝乙的妾，后来才立为正妻生了纣，于是纣获得立嗣的正统地位而继承了帝位，微子则封为子爵，成了纣王的卿士。纣王无道，微子屡谏不听，遂隐居荒野。周武王灭殷后， 被封于宋。

2 箕子：名胥馀，殷纣王的叔父。他的采邑在箕（在今山西省太谷县东北）。子爵，官太师。曾多次劝说纣王，纣王不听，箕子披发装疯，被纣王拘囚，降为奴隶。周武王灭殷后才被释放。

3 比干：殷纣王的叔父。官少师，屡次竭力强谏纣王并表明“主过不谏，非忠也；畏死不言，非勇也；

礼堕三都 Pulling Down Three City Walls According to Ritual

过则谏，不用则死，忠之至也。”纣王大怒，竟说：“吾闻圣人之心有七窍，信诸？”（《史记·殷本纪》注引《括地志》）遂将比干剖胸挖心，残忍地杀死。

【英译文】

Under the tyranny of King Zhou of the Yin Dynasty, Wei Zi (the king's elder brother) fled from him, Qi Zi (the king's uncle) suffered slavery at his hands, and Bi Gan was put to death because he remonstrated with the king. The Master said, "The three of them were virtuous men of Yin."

18.2

柳下惠为士师[1]，三黜[2]。人曰：“子未可以去乎[3]？”曰：“直道而事人，焉往而不三黜[4]？枉道而事人[5]，何必去父母之邦[6]？”

【中译文】

柳下惠担任司法官，多次被免职。有人说：“您为什么不离开呢？”柳下惠说：“正直地事奉人君，到哪一国去不会被多次免职？如果不正直地事奉人君，何必要离开自己的家国呢？”

【注释】

1 士师：古代掌管司法刑狱的官员。

2 三黜（chù）：多次被罢免。“三”，表示多次，不一定只有三次。

3 去：离开。

4 焉：代词，表疑问。哪里。往：去。

5 枉：不正。

6 父母之邦：父母所在之国，即本国，祖国。

齐景公待孔子曰：“若季氏，则吾不能；以季孟之间待之。”曰：“吾老矣，不能用也。”孔子行1。

【英译文】

When Liuxia Hui was three times deposed from his position in charge of penalties, someone said to him, "Can't you make up your mind to leave the state?" But he said, "If I am to serve men uprightly, where could I go and not be deposed three times? If I am to serve men dishonestly, why must I leave my native state?"

18.3

齐景公待孔子曰：“若季氏，则吾不能；以季孟之间待之。”曰：“吾老矣，不能用也。”孔子行[1]。

【中译文】

齐景公讲到对待孔子的规格说：“若像鲁国国君对待季氏那样来对待他，我做不到；可以用比季孙氏低比孟孙氏高的待遇来对待他。”后来齐景公又说：“我老了，不能用他了。’孔子便动身离开了。

【注释】

1 孔子行：公元前509年，孔子到齐国，想得到齐景公的重用；结果，有人反对，甚至扬言要杀孔子。齐景公迫于压力，不敢任用，孔子于是离开齐国。

【英译文】

When speaking of how to treat Confucius, Duke Jing of Qi said, "To treat him equally with the head of the Ji Family as the king of Lu did is impossible. I will treat him as ranking between the Ji and Meng Families." Later he said, "I am too old to undertake the reforms. So I can't use him." The Master then left the land of Qi.

18.4

齐人归女乐[1]，季桓子受之[2]，三日不朝，孔子行[3]。

【中译文】

齐国人赠送了许多歌姬舞女给鲁国，季桓子接受了，三天不上朝。孔子便离开了鲁国。

【注释】

1 归：同“馈”。赠送。

2 季桓子：鲁国贵族，姓季孙，名斯，季孙肥（康子）的父亲。从鲁定公时至鲁哀公初年，一直担任鲁国执政的上卿（宰相）。

3 孔子行：《史记·孔子世家》：“定公十四年，孔子为鲁司寇，摄行相事。齐人惧，归（馈）女乐以沮（阻止）之。”孔子看到鲁国君臣这样迷恋女乐，朝政日衰，不足有为，便大大失望而去职离鲁。

【英译文】

The people of Qi sent Lu dancing girls as presents (in order to weaken the power of the government), and Ji Huanzi accepted them. For three days no court was held. The Master then left.

18.5

楚狂接舆歌而过孔子曰[1]：“凤兮[2]！凤兮！何德之衰？往者不可谏[3]，来者犹可追[4]。已而，已而，今之从政者殆而[5]。”孔子下，欲与之言。趋而辟之[6]，不得与之言。

【中译文】

楚国狂人接舆经过孔子的车旁，唱到：“凤凰呀！凤凰呀！为什么道德这么衰微？过去的事不可挽回了，未来的事还来得及改正。算了吧，算了吧，如今从政的人危险啊。”孔子下车想同他交谈。他却快步避开了，孔子没能同他说话。

【注释】

1 接舆：“接”，迎。“舆”，车。迎面遇着孔子的

车。这里因其事而呼其人为“接舆”。传说乃楚国人，是“躬耕以食”的隐者贤士，用唱歌来批评时政，被世人视为狂人。一说，接舆本姓陆，名通，字接舆。见楚昭王政事无常，乃佯狂不仕，于是被人们看做 是楚国的一个疯子。

2 凤：凤凰。古时传说，世有道则凤鸟见，无道则隐。这里比喻孔子。接舆认为孔子世无道而不能隐，故 说“德衰”。

3 谏：规劝，使改正错误。

4 犹可追：尚可补救，还来得及改正。

5 而：语助词，相当于“矣”。

6 辟：同“避”。

【英译文】

Jie Yu, the madman of Chu (he was in fact a hermit), sang as he passed by Confucius, "Oh phoenix (Confucius is probably compared to the phoenix), how dwindled is your power! It is impossible to retrieve what has passed, but the future may yet be remedied. Desist! Desist! Those who are in power today are dangerous."

The Master (Confucius) got out of his carriage and wished to talk with him, but the man fled quickly. The Master did not succeed in speaking to him.

18.6

长沮、桀溺耦而耕[1]，孔子过之，使子路问津焉。

长沮曰：“夫执舆者为谁[2]？”子路曰：“为孔丘。”曰：“是鲁孔丘与[3]？”曰：“是也。”曰：“是知津矣。”

问于桀溺。桀溺曰：“子为谁？”曰：“为仲由。”曰：“是鲁孔丘之徒与？”对曰：“然。”曰：“滔滔者天下皆是也，而谁以易之？且而与其从辟人之士也[4]，岂若从辟世之士哉[5]。”耰而不辍[6]。

子路行以告。夫子怃然曰[7]：“鸟兽不可与同群，吾非斯人之徒与而谁与[8]？天下有道，丘不与易也[9]。”

【中译文】

长沮、桀溺两人一起耕田，孔子从旁经过，让子路去打听渡口。长沮说：“那驾车的人是谁？”子路说：“是孔丘。”长沮说：“是鲁国的孔丘吗？”子路说：“是的。”长沮说：“那他自己该知道渡口在哪里。”子路又去问桀溺。桀溺说：“您是谁？”子路说：“是仲由。”桀溺说：“是鲁国孔丘的徒弟吗？”子路回答：“是的。”桀溺说：“天下大乱就像滔滔的洪水泛滥，谁能改变这种现状呢？而且，你与其跟随躲避坏人的人，还不如跟随避开世事的人呢。”边说边耕种着。子路回来告诉孔子。孔子颇为惆怅说：“人与鸟兽是不可同群的，我不同世人一起生活又同谁呢？假若天下有道，我孔丘

就不参与变革了。”

【注释】

1 长沮：桀溺：“长”，个头高大。“沮（jù）”，沮洳，泥水润泽之处。“桀”，同“杰”。身材魁梧。“溺”，身浸水中。这是两位在泥水中从事劳动的隐者。长沮、桀溺，都是形容人的形象，不是真实姓名。耦（ǒu）：二人合耕，各执一耜（sì），左右并发。

2 执舆者：驾车的人。此指孔子。本来是子路驾车的，因下车问津，所以由孔子代为驾车，孔子便成了“执舆者”。

3 与：通“欤”。吗。

4 且：而且。而：同“尔”。你。辟人之士：躲避人的人。指孔子。孔子离开鲁国，到处奔波，躲避与自己志趣不合的人，不同他们合作，故称。“辟”，同“避”。

5 辟世之士：避开整个社会的隐士。

6 耰（yōu）：古代农具，用来击碎土块和平整土地。这里指用耰翻土去覆盖种子。辍（chuò）：停止，中止。

7 怃（wǔ）然：怅惘失意的样子。

8 斯人之徒：指世上的人们，现实社会的那些从政者，统治者。

9 与：相与，参与。易：变易，改革。

【英译文】

Chang Ju and Jie Ni were working together in the fields. The Master, happening to pass that way, told Zi Lu to go and ask them where the fording place was.

Chang Ju asked, "Who is that holding the reins?" "It's Confucius."

"Do you mean Confucius of Lu?"

"Yes." "He should know the fording place (for he claims to be a sage)."

Zi Lu then asked Jie Ni ,who replied, "Who are you?" "I am Zhong You(i. e., Zi Lu)."

"Are you a pupil of Confucius?"

"Yes." "Disorder, like a swelling flood, spreads everywhere, and with whom will you change it? Instead of following one who flees from bad men, you would do better to join us who flee from the world." And with that he went on covering the seed.

Zi Lu went back and told the Master.

The Master said disappointedly, "We cannot herd with birds and beasts. If I do not associate with these people, with whom shall I associate? If the world were following the right way, I should not be doing my part to reform it."

18.7

子路从而后，遇丈人[1]，以杖荷蓧[2]。子路问：“子见夫子乎？”丈人曰：“四体不勤，五谷不分，孰为夫子？”植其杖而芸[3]。子路拱而立。止子路宿，杀鸡为黍而食之[4]，见其二子焉。明日，子路行以告。子曰：“隐者也。”使子路反见之[5]，至则行矣。

5 反：同“返”。返回去。

【英译文】

As Zi Lu was traveling with Confucius, he once fell behind and met with an old man carrying some tool for weeding over his shoulder by means of his walking stick.

Zi Lu asked him, "Have you ever seen my Master?"

The old man said, "He's a man who does no physical work and can't tell one kind of grain from another. How can he be your master?" With that he set down his stick and began weeding. While Zi Lu stood by with his hands pressed together. The old man kept Zi Lu for the night, killed a chicken and prepared a dish of millet for his supper and introduced him to his sons.

The following day, Zi Lu went on his way and reported the matter to his master. The Master said. "He is a hermit." Then he told Zi Lu to go back and visit him again. But on arriving at the place he found that the old man had gone away. (Perhaps he feared that Confucius might recommend him for pubic office.)

Thereupon Zi Lu said, "It is not right to refuse to take office. Just as the laws of age and youth must be preserved, so must the right relation between the prince and subject be maintained. Desire to maintain one's own personal integrity can lead to the disruption of a greater principle. A gentleman takes office in the government so as to do what is righteous. It has long been known that the right way does not prevail."

18.8

逸民[1]：伯夷，叔齐，虞仲[2]，夷逸[3]，朱张[4]，柳下惠，少连[5]。子曰：“不降其志，不辱其身，伯夷、叔齐与！”谓：“柳下惠、少连，降

子路曰：“不仕无义。长幼之节不可废也，君臣之义如之何其废之？欲洁其身而乱大伦。君子之仕也，行其义也。道之不行，已知之矣。”

【中译文】

子路跟随孔子，途中落在后面。遇见一位老人，用木杖挑着除草的农具。子路问：“您看见我的老师了吗？”老人说：“你们四肢不劳动，五谷分不清，谁知哪个是你老师？”接着把木杖插在地上，除草去了。子路拱手站在一旁。老人留子路到他家住宿，杀鸡、做黍米饭给子路吃，并让两个儿子见了子路。第二天，子路赶上了孔子，告诉了这件事。孔子说：“这是位隐士。”让子路返回去看老人。子路到了那里，老人已经走了。子路说：“不事奉无义的君主。长幼之间的礼节不可废弃，君臣之义如何能废弃呢？只想洁身自好，却乱了君臣间大的伦理关系是不对的。但君子之所以要从政做官，就是为了实行君臣之义。至于道义行不通，我们早就知道了。”

【注释】

1 丈人：老人。姓名身世不详。一说，楚国叶县人。

2 荷（hè）：挑，担，扛。蓧（diào）：古代一种竹制农具。用以除草。

3 芸：同“耘”。除草。

4 食（sì）：拿东西给别人吃。

志辱身矣，言中伦[6]，行中虑，其斯而已矣。"谓："虞仲、夷逸，隐居放言，身中清，废中权。我则异于是，无可无不可[7]。"

【中译文】

逸民有：伯夷、叔齐、虞仲、夷逸、朱张、柳下惠、少连。孔子说："不放弃自己的志向，不辱没自己的身份，就是伯夷、叔齐吧！"又说："柳下惠、少连，被迫放弃自己的志向，辱没自己的身份，但说话合乎伦理，行为深思熟虑，他们只是这样做而已啊。"又说："虞仲、夷逸，避世隐居而言论清高，洁身自好而处事灵活。可是我与这些人不同，没有什么可以，也没有什么不可以。"

【注释】

1 逸民：隐退不仕的人，失去政治、经济地位的贵族。

2 虞仲：即仲雍，为推辞王位，与兄泰伯一同隐至荆蛮。见《泰伯篇第八》第一章注。一说，是《史记》中吴君周章之弟。

3 夷逸：古代隐士。自称是牛，可耕于野，而不忍被诱入庙而为牺牲。

4 朱张：字子弓。身世不详。

5 少连：东夷人。善于守孝，达于礼。

6 中(zhòng)：符合，合于。

7 "无可"句：意思是说：根据客观实际情况的发展变化而考虑怎样做适宜。得时则驾，随遇而安。《孟子·万章下》说：孔子是"圣之时者也"，"可以速而速，可以久而久，可以处而处，可以仕而仕"。随机应变，见机行事。不一定这样做，也不一定不这样做。

【英译文】

The men who had retired to privacy from the society were Bo Yi, Shu Qi, Yu Zhong, Yi Yi, Zhu Zhang, Liuxia Hui and Shao Lian. The Master said of them, "Bo Yi and Shu Qi would neither abate their high reputation nor bring humiliation upon themselves." Of Liuxia Hui and Shao Lian he said, "They did abate their high resolve and bring humiliation upon themselves, but they spoke in accord with high principles and acted after consideration. This and no more." Of Yu Zhong and Yi Yi he said, "They lived in seclusion and refrained from comment. They secured personal integrity and their abstention from public office was in keeping with prevailing conditions. As for me, I am different from any of these. I takes life as it comes."

18.9

太师挚适齐[1]，亚饭干适楚[2]，三饭缭适蔡，四饭缺适秦；鼓方叔入于河[3]，播鼗武入于汉[4]；少师阳、击磬襄[5]，入于海。

【中译文】

太师挚去了齐国，亚饭乐师干去了楚国，三饭乐师缭去了蔡国，四饭乐师缺去了秦国；打鼓的方叔去了黄河地区，摇小鼓的武去了汉水地区；少师阳和击磬的襄，去了海滨。鲁国之乐衰微了。

【注释】

1 太师挚：可能就是《泰伯篇第八》第十五章中所说的“师挚”，是乐官之长。可参阅。

2 亚饭：按周朝制度规定，天子和诸侯吃饭时要奏乐。“亚饭”是第二次吃饭时奏乐的乐师，“三饭”、“四饭”依此类推。干：及下文“缭”、“缺”，均为乐师名。

3 鼓方叔：打鼓的乐师，名方叔。河：专指黄河。

4 播：摇。鼗（táo）：长柄摇鼓，两旁系有小槌。武：是摇小鼓的乐师的名子。

5 少师阳：乐官之佐（副乐师），名阳。击磬襄：敲磬的乐师，名襄。孔子曾向他学琴。以上这些鲁国的乐师流亡四方，各找出路，说明鲁公室已日益衰微。

【英译文】

The chief musician Zhi left and went to the state of Qi; Gan, the one who played at the second meal of the day, went to Chu; Liao, the one who played at the third meal, went to Cai; Que, the musician at the fourth meal, went to Qin; Fang Shu, the drum-beater, went north of the Yellow River; Wu, the twirler of the hand drum, went down into the valley of the Han River; the assistant musicians Yang and Xiang, the players of stone-chimes, went out to live near the sea.

18.10

周公谓鲁公曰[1]：“君子不施其亲[2]，不使大臣怨乎不以[3]；故旧无大故，则不弃也；无求备于一人。”

【中译文】

周公对鲁公说：“君子不能疏远亲人，不能让大臣抱怨不被任用；老人，如果没有重大的过错，不要抛弃；对人不要求全责备。”

【注释】

1 周公：武王之弟，名姬旦。鲁公：指周公的儿子伯禽。

2 施：同“弛“。松弛，放松，弃置。引申为疏远，怠慢。

3 以：用，任用。

【英译文】

The Duke of Zhou said to the Duke of Lu, A gentleman never discards his kinsmen; nor does he ever give occasion to his chief retainers to chafe at not being used. None who have been long in his service does he ever dismiss without grave cause. He does not expect one man to be capable of doing everything.

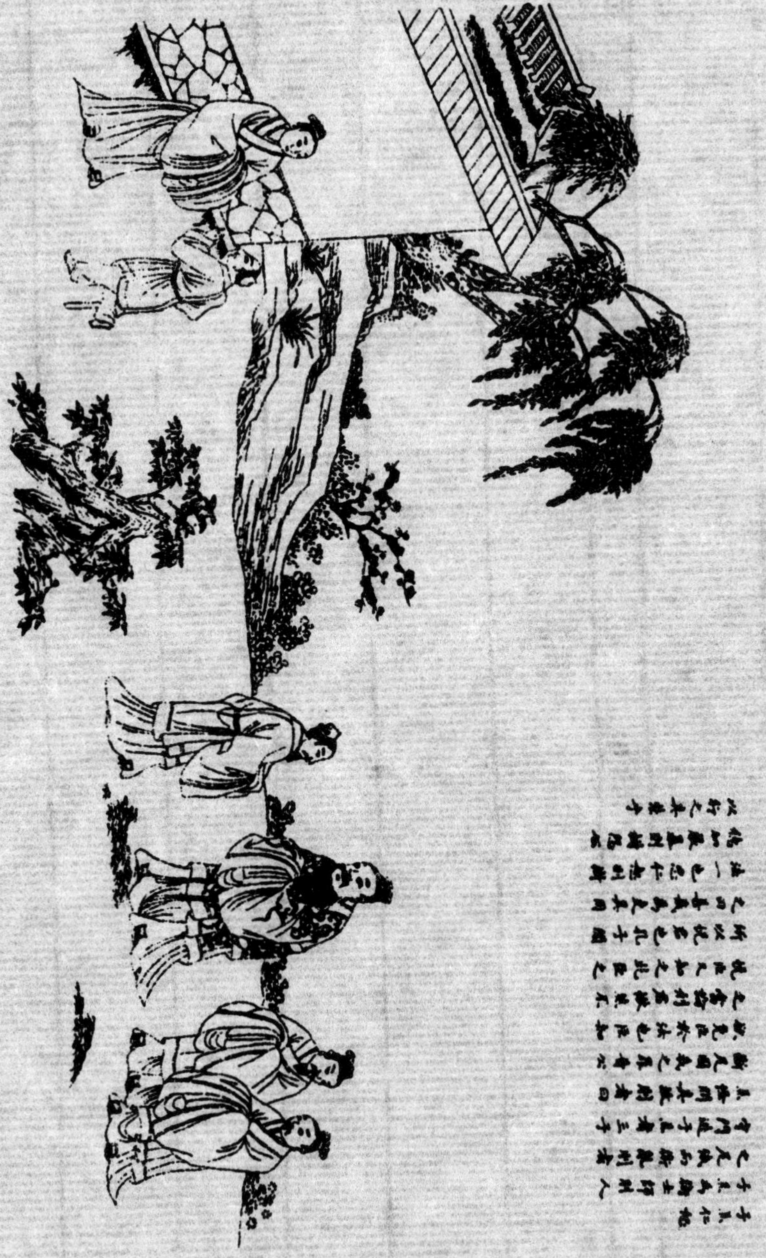

The Compassion and Benevolence of Zigao

18.11

周有八士[1]：伯达，伯适，仲突，仲忽，叔夜，叔夏，季随，季騧。

【中译文】

周朝有八位名士：伯达，伯适，仲突，仲忽，叔夜，叔夏，季随，季騧。

【注释】

1 八士：身世生平不详。或说，周初盛时，有这八名才德之士：伯达通达义理，伯适（kuò）大度能容，仲突有御难之才，仲忽有综理之才，叔夜柔顺不迫，叔夏刚明不屈，季随有应顺之才能，季騧（guā）德同良马。八人都很有教养，有贤名。或传说八士为一母所生的四对孪生子（见《逸周书》）。

【英译文】

Under the Zhou Dynasty there were eight gentlemen. They were Bo Da, Bo Kuo, Zhong Tu, Zhong Hu, Shu Ye, Shu Xia, Ji Sui and Ji Gua.

18.11

周有八士[1]：伯达，伯适，仲突，仲忽，叔夜，叔夏，季随，季騧。

【中译文】

周朝有八位名士：伯达，伯适，仲突，仲忽，叔夜，叔夏，季随，季騧。

【注释】

1 八士：身世生平不详。或说，周初盛时，有这八名才德之士：伯达通达文理，伯适（kuò）大度能容，仲突有御难之才，仲忽有综理之才，叔夜柔顺不迫，叔夏刚明不屈，季随有应顺之才能，季騧（guā）德同良马。八人都很有教养，有贤名。或传说八士为一母所生的四对孪生子（见《逸周书》）。

【英译文】

Under the Zhou Dynasty there were eight gentlemen. They were Bo Da, Bo Kuo, Zhong Tu, Zhong Hu, Shu Ye, Shu Xia, Ji Sui and Ji Gua.

The Compassion and Benevolence of Zigao

子张篇第十九（共二十五章）

The Students£§Respect for Confucius

19.1

子张曰：“士见危致命[1]，见得思义[2]，祭思敬，丧思哀，其可已矣[3]。”

【中译文】

子张说：“知识分子遇见危难可以献出自己生命；遇见利益能考虑是否合乎义；祭祀时，能想到恭敬严肃；临丧时，能想到悲哀。这样做就可以了。”

【注释】

1 致命：授命，舍弃生命。

2 思：反省，考虑。

3 其可已矣：“见危致命，见得思义，祭思敬，丧思哀”这四方面是立身之大节。作为知识分子，如能做到这些，就算可以了。

【英译文】

Zi Zhang said, A knight who confronted with danger is ready to lay down his life, who confronted with the chance of gain thinks first of right, who judges sacrifice by the degree of reverence shown and mourning by the degree of grief-such a one is all that can be desired.

19.2

子张曰：“执德不弘[1]，信道不笃，焉能为有？焉能为亡[2]？”

【中译文】

子张问：“执守仁德不能发扬光大，信仰道义不能固守不变，这样怎么算有仁德，又怎么算一点道义都没有？”

【注释】

1 弘：弘扬，发扬光大。一说：“弘”即今之“强”字，坚强，坚定不移（见章炳麟《广论语骈枝》）。

2 “焉能”句：意谓无足轻重；有他不为多，无他不为少；有他没他一个样。“亡”，同“无”。

【英译文】

Zi Zhang said, He who maintains virtue and morality, but only to a limited extent, who believes in the Way, but without conviction-how can one count him as with us, how can one count him as not with us?

19.3

子夏之门人问交于子张。子张曰：“子夏云何？”对曰：“子夏曰：‘可者与之，其不可者拒之。’”子张曰：“异乎吾所闻：君子尊贤而容众，嘉善而矜不能[1]。我之大贤与[2]，于人何

19.4

子夏曰："虽小道[1]，必有可观者焉，致远恐泥[2]，是以君子不为也。"

【中译文】

子夏说："虽是小的技艺，也一定有可取之道，但要从事远大的事业，便不能陷在其中，所以君子不专门掌握这些小技艺。"

【注释】

1 小道：指某一方面的技能，技艺，如古代所谓农、圃、医、卜、乐、百工之类。

2 泥（nì）：不通达，留滞，拘泥。

【英译文】

Zi Xia said, "Even the minor crafts have an importance of their own. But they tend to prove a hindrance to lofty ideals. For that reason, a gentleman does not pursue them."

19.5

子夏曰："日知其所亡[1]，月无忘其所能，可谓好学也已矣。"

【中译文】

子夏说："每天知道一些新知识，每月不忘记已经

所不容？我之不贤与，人将拒我，如之何其拒人也？"

【中译文】

子夏的学生向子张请教交友之道。子张问："子夏是怎样说的？"回答："子夏说：'可交的就与他交往，不可交的就拒绝交往。'"子张说："这和我听说的不同：君子能尊敬贤人，又能容纳众人；能赞美好人，又能怜悯能力差的人。我如果是很贤明的，对于别人为何不能容纳呢？我如果不贤明，别人将会拒绝我，如何谈得上拒绝别人呢？"

【注释】

1 矜（jīn）：怜悯，怜恤，同情。

2 与：同"欤"。语气词。

【英译文】

A disciple of Zi Xia asked Zi Zhang about friendship. Zi Zhang said, "What does Zi Xia say on the subject?" He replied saying, "Zi Xia says: 'Make friends with those you approve and reject those whom you disapprove'." Zi Zhang said, "That differs from what I was taught. A gentleman respects men of the highest caliber, but maintains a proper regard for all. He commends the good and pities the incapable. If I am a man of the highest caliber, I shall certainly maintain a proper regard for all. If not, my fellowmen will reject me. How can I reject my fellowmen?"

掌握的，就可以称为好学的人了。”

【注释】

1 亡：同“无”。这里指自己所没有的知识、技能，所不懂的道理等。

【英译文】

Zi Xia said, He who from day to day is conscious of what he still lacks, and from month to month never forgets what he has already learnt, may indeed be called a true lover of learning.

19.6

子夏曰：“博学而笃志，切问而近思，仁在其中矣。”

【中译文】

子夏说：“广博地学习钻研，坚定自己的志向，恳切地提问，联系当前实际思考，仁德就在其中了。’

【英译文】

Zi Xia said, one who studies widely and with set purpose, who questions earnestly, then thinks for himself about what he has heard such a one will incidentally achieve Goodness.

19.7

子夏曰：“百工居肆以成其事[1]，君子学以致

其道。”

【中译文】

子夏说：“各行业的工匠在作坊里完成他们的工作，君子通过求学达到实现道的目的。”

【注释】

1 肆：古代制造物品的场所。如官府营造器物的地方，手工业作坊。陈列商品的店铺，也叫肆。

【英译文】

Zi Xia said, Just as the hundred workmen must live in workshops to perfect themselves in their craft, so the gentleman studies, that he may improve himself in the Way.

19.8

子夏曰：“小人之过也必文。”

【中译文】

子夏说：“小人的过错，必定自我掩饰。”

【英译文】

Zi Xia said, A petty man always glosses over his faults.

19.9

子夏曰："君子有三变：望之俨然，即之也温，听其言也厉。"

【中译文】

子夏说："君子的态度让你感到有三种变化：远看外表庄严可畏，接近他和蔼可亲，听他说的话准确犀利。"

【英译文】

Zi Xia said, A gentleman has three varying aspects: seen from afar, he looks severe, when approached he is found to be mild, when heard speaking he turns out to be incisive.

19.10

子夏曰："君子信而后劳其民[1]；未信，则以为厉己也[2]。信而后谏；未信，则以为谤己也。"

【中译文】

子夏说："君子要先取得百姓的信任，而后再役使他们；否则百姓就会以为是虐待他们。对君主要先取得信任而后去劝谏；否则君主就会以为是诽谤自己。"

【注释】

1 劳：指役使，让百姓去服劳役。

2 厉：虐待，折磨，坑害。

【英译文】

Zi Xia said, A gentleman obtains the confidence of those under him, before putting burdens upon them. If he does so before he has obtained their confidence, they feel that they are being exploited. It is also true that he obtains the confidence(of those above him) before criticiszing them. If he does so before he has obtained their confidence, they feel that they are being slandered.

19.11

子夏曰："大德不逾闲[1]，小德出入可也。"

【中译文】

子夏说："在德操大节上不要超越界限，在细微小节上有点出入是可以的。"

【注释】

1 大德：与下"小德"相对，犹言大节。小德即小节。一般认为，大德指纲常伦理方面的节操。小德指日常的生活作风，礼貌，仪表，待人接物，言语文词等。逾：超越，越过。闲：本义是阑，栅栏。引申为限制，界限，法度。

【英译文】

Zi Xia said, So long as in undertakings of great moral import a man does not 'cross the barrier', in undertakings of little moral import he may 'come out

and go in'.

19.12

子游曰：“子夏之门人小子，当洒扫应对进退，则可矣，抑末也[1]。本之则无，如之何？”

子夏闻之，曰：“噫！言游过矣！君子之道[2]，孰先传焉？孰后倦焉[3]？譬诸草木，区以别矣。君子之道，焉可诬也？有始有卒者，其惟圣人乎！”

【中译文】

子游说：“子夏的学生，做些洒水扫地接待迎送的事是可以的，但这不过是末节。根本的东西却没有学到，这怎么行呢？”子夏听了这些话，说：“唉！子游错了！君子之道，哪些先传授，哪些后传授呢？就像草木，其门类是有区别的。君子之道，怎么可以诬蔑歪曲呢？能够有始有终，由洒扫进退到知书识礼的，大概只有圣人吧！”

【注释】

1 抑：抑或，或许。末：非根本的方法，末节。

2 君子之道：指君子的立身之道。与“本”有密切联系，故《论语》有“君子务本，本立而道生”的话。

3 “孰先”句：句中“倦”字，当是“传”字之误，一说“倦”字不误，意思是：君子之道，传于人，宜有先后，非以其“末”为先而传之，非以其“本”为后而倦教，非专传其宜先者，而倦传其宜后者。

【英译文】

Zi You said, "Zi Xia's disciples know how to sprinkle and sweep, how to answer summonses and reply to questions, how to come forward and retire. But these are small matters. They are lacking in the fundamentals. What can we do with them?"

Zi Xia, hearing of this, said, "Alas, Zi You is wholly mistaken. Of the ways of a gentleman, which is to be transmitted first or second should be separately treated, just as plants and trees should be separately treated according to their kinds. How can the ways of a gentleman be misrepresented? It is only the sage who can transmit knowledge systematically." just as plants and trees should be separately treated according to their kinds. How can the ways of a gentleman be misrepresented? It is only the sage who can transmit knowledge systematically."

19.13

子夏曰：“仕而优则学[1]，学而优则仕。”

【中译文】

子夏说：“做官要做得好就应该进一步学习；学习好了就可以出来做官。”

【注释】

1 优：优秀，优良。一说：“优”，充足，富裕。

国为民尽职尽责，有馀力，便应学习（资其仕者益深）；为学的首先是明道修德掌握知识技能，有馀力，则可做官（验其学者益广）。

【英译文】

Zi Xia said, "An official has to study constantly if he wants to do his duty well. On the other hand, if one wants to be an official, he has to study well."

19.14

子游曰："丧致乎哀而止[1]。"

【中译文】

子游说："居丧时能够表达悲哀之情就可以了。"

【注释】

1 "丧致乎"句：这句话包含两层含意：一、居丧尚有悲哀之情，而不尚繁礼文饰。二、既已哀，则当止，不当过哀以至毁身灭性。"丧"，指在直系亲长丧期之中。

【英译文】

Zi You said, "Let mourning stop after the grief is fully expressed."

19.15

子游曰："吾友张也为难能也[1]，然而未

仁。"

【中译文】

子游说："我的朋友子张，是难能可贵的人物，然而还没达到仁。"

【注释】

1 张：即颛孙师，字子张。朱熹说："子张行过高，而少诚实恻怛之意。"才高意广，人所难能，而心驰于外，不能全其心德，未得为仁。

【英译文】

Zi You said, "My friend Zi Zhang is capable of many difficult things, but he is not yet perfectly virtuous."

19.16

曾子曰："堂堂乎张也[1]，难与并为仁矣。"

【中译文】

曾子说："仪表堂堂的子张啊，别人很难同他一起学习与体认仁的境界呀。"

【注释】

1 堂堂：形容仪表壮伟，气派十足。据说子张外有余而内不足，他的为人重在"言语形貌"，不重在"正心诚意"，故人不能助他为仁，他也不能助人为仁。

【英译文】

Zeng Zi said, Zi Zhang is so self-important. It is hard to become Good when working together with such a man.

19.17

曾子曰："吾闻诸夫子，人未有自致者也[1]，必也亲丧乎！"

【中译文】

曾子说："我听老师说过，人没有完全自动表露内心真情的，只有在父母去世才可能吧！"

【注释】

1 致：极，尽。这里指充分表露和发泄内心全部的真实感情。父母之丧，哀痛迫切之情，不待人勉而自尽其极。

【英译文】

Zeng Zi said, I once heard the Master say, Though a man may never before have shown all that is in him, he is certain to do so when mourning for a parent.

19.18

曾子曰："吾闻诸夫子：孟庄子之孝也[1]，其他可能也，其不改父之臣与父之政，是难能

也。"

【中译文】

曾子说："我听老师说过：孟庄子行孝，其他方面别人也能做到，但不更换父亲的旧臣，不改变父亲的治政措施，却是别人难以做到的。"

【注释】

1 孟庄子：鲁国大夫孟孙速。其父是孟孙蔑（孟献子），品德好，有贤名。

【英译文】

Zeng Zi said, I once heard the Master say, Filial piety such as that of Meng Zhuangzi might in other respects be possible to imitate; but the way in which he changed neither his father's servants nor his father's domestic policy, would indeed be hard to emulate.

19.19

孟氏使阳肤为士师[1]。问于曾子。曾子曰："上失其道，民散久矣。如得其情，则哀矜而勿喜[2]！"

【中译文】

孟孙氏任命阳肤做法官。阳肤征求曾子意见。曾子说："当政者背离正道，百姓人心已散很久了。如果

掌握了百姓犯罪实情，应当同情怜悯他们，而不要因能理狱而暗自高兴。”

【注释】

1 阳肤：相传是曾参七名弟子中的一名。武城人。

2 矜：怜悯，怜惜，同情。

【英译文】

When Meng Sun appointed Yang Fu as Leader of the Knights, Yang Fu came for advice to Zeng Zi. Zeng Zi said, It is long since those above lost the Way of the Ruler and the common people lost their cohesion. If you find evidence of this, you should be sad and show pity rather than be pleased at discovering such evidence.

19.20

子贡曰：“纣之不善[1]，不如是之甚也[2]。是以君子恶居下流[3]，天下之恶皆归焉[4]。”

【中译文】

子贡说：“殷纣王的不善，不如传说中的那样过分。所以君子不宜因品行而使自己处于不利的位置，如果那样，天下的一切坏事坏名都会归到他的头上来。”

【注释】

1 纣：名辛，史称“帝辛”，“纣”是谥号（按照谥法，残忍不义称为“纣”）。商朝最后一个君主，是历史上有名的暴君。据史料看，纣有文武才能，对东方的开发，对文化的发展和中国的统一，都曾有过贡献。但他宠爱妲己，贪酒好色，刚愎自用，拒纳忠言。制定残酷的刑法，压制人民。又大兴土木，无休止地役使人民。后周武王会合西南各族向纣进攻，牧野（今河南淇县西南）一战，纣兵败，逃入城内，引火自焚而死。殷遂灭。

2 是：代词。指人们传说的那样。

3 恶（wù）：讨厌，憎恨，憎恶。下流：地势卑下处。这里指由高位而降至低位。

4 恶（è）：坏事，罪恶。子贡说这番话的意思，当然不是为纣王去辩解开脱，而是要提醒世人（尤其是当权者），应当经常自我警戒反省，在台上的时候律己要严。否则一旦失势，置身“下流”，天下的“恶名”将集于一身而遗臭万年。

【英译文】

Zi Gong said, The King Zhou in the Yin Dynasty cannot really have been as wicked as all this! That is why a gentleman hates to do anything bad. He knows that all filth under Heaven tends to accumulate there.

19.21

子贡曰：“君子之过也，如日月之食焉[1]：过也，人皆见之；更也[2]，人皆仰之。”

【中译文】

子贡说："君子的过错，如同日蚀月蚀：过错，人们都看得见；更改，人们都仰敬。

【注释】

1 食：同"蚀"。

2 更：变更，更改。

【英译文】

Zi Gong said, The faults of a gentleman are like eclipses of the sun or moon. If he does wrong, everyone sees it. When he corrects his fault, every gaze is turned up towards him.

19.22

卫公孙朝问于子贡曰[1]："仲尼焉学？"子贡曰："文武之道，未坠于地[2]，在人。贤者识其大者，不贤者识其小者，莫不有文武之道焉。夫子焉不学？而亦何常师之有[3]？"

【中译文】

卫国的公孙朝问子贡："仲尼的学问是从哪学来的？"子贡说："周文王、周武王之道，并未失传，还在世间流传。贤人知道大的方面，不贤的人知道小的方面，无处不有文武之道。我的老师何处不学呢？又可曾有固定的老师呢？"

【注释】

1 公孙朝：卫国大夫。

2 坠于地：掉到地下。这里指被人们轻视而遗弃，被人遗忘，失传。

3 常师：固定的老师。子贡说孔子不是专向某一个人学习，而是向众人学习。传说孔子曾经向礼于老聃（dān），访乐于长弘，问官于郯子，学琴于师襄。故唐代韩愈说"圣人无常师"（见《师说》）。

【英译文】

Gongsun Chao of Wei asked Zi Gong, From whom did the Master derive his learning? Zi Gong said, The Way of the kings Wen and Wu has never yet utterly fallen to the ground. Among men, those of great understanding have recorded the major principles of this Way and those of less understanding have recorded the minor principles. So that there is no one who has not access to the Way of Wen and Wu. From whom indeed did our Master not learn? But at the same time, what need had he of any fixed and regular teacher?

19.23

叔孙武叔语大夫于朝曰[1]："子贡贤于仲尼。"

子服景伯以告子贡[2]。

子贡曰："譬之宫墙[3]，赐之墙也及肩，窥见室家之好。夫子之墙数仞[4]，不得其门而入，不见宗庙之美，百官之富[5]。得其门者或寡矣。夫

good points of the house on the other side. But our Master's wall rises many times a man's height, and no one who is not let in by the gate can know the beauty and wealth of the palace that, with its ancestral temple its hundred ministrants, lies hidden within. But it must be admitted that those who are let in by the gate are few; so that it is small wonder His Excellency should have spoken like that.

19.24

叔孙武叔毁仲尼。子贡曰："无以为也！仲尼不可毁也。他人之贤者，丘陵也，犹可逾也；仲尼，日月也，无得而逾焉。人虽欲自绝[1]，其何伤于日月乎？多见其不知量也[2]。"

【中译文】

叔孙武叔毁谤仲尼。子贡说："不要这样做啊！仲尼是不可毁谤的。别的贤人，如丘陵，还可以跨越过去；仲尼，如日月，是无法越过的。有人想要自绝于日月，对日月有什么损伤呢？只不过太不自量力啊。"

【注释】

1 自绝：自行断绝跟对方之间的关系。
2 多：只是，徒然，恰好是。不知量：不知自己的分量，不知高低轻重，不自量。

【英译文】

When Shu sun Wu shu spoke evil of the Master, Zi Gong said, It is no use;

子之云，不亦宜乎[6]！"

【中译文】

叔孙武叔在朝廷上对大夫们说："子贡比孔子贤良。"子服景伯转告给了子贡。子贡说："用围墙作个比喻吧，我的围墙，只够到肩膀那么高，站在墙外，人们都能窥见房屋的美好。我老师的围墙有几丈高，找不到门，无法进去，看不到宗庙的美好和各个房舍的繁富。能找到门进去的人或许还很少呢。叔孙武叔老先生那样说，不也是与此相像吗！"

【注释】

1 叔孙武叔：鲁国大夫，"三桓"之一，名州仇。
2 子服景伯：名何，鲁国大夫。
3 宫：房屋，住舍。古代不论尊卑贵贱，住所都称"宫"。到了秦代才专称帝王的住所为宫。
4 仞（rèn）：古代长度，七尺（或说八尺）叫一仞。
5 官：本义是房舍，后来才引申为做官，官职。这里用本义。
6 宜：适宜，相称，很自然。

【英译文】

Shu sun Wu shu said to some high officers at Court, Zi Gong is a better man than the Master. Zi Fu Jing Bo repeated this to Zi Gong. Zi Gong said, Let us take as our comparison the wall round a building. My wall only reaches to the level of a man's shoulder, and it is easy enough to peep over it and see the

the Master cannot be disparaged. There may be other good men; but they are merely like hillocks or mounds that can easily be climbed. The Master is the sun and moon that cannot be climbed over. If a man should try to cut himself off from them, what harm would it do to the sun and moon? It would only show that he did not know his own measure.

19.25

陈子禽谓子贡曰[1]：“子为恭也，仲尼岂贤于子乎？”子贡曰：“君子一言以为知[2]，一言以为不知，言不可不慎也。夫子之不可及也，犹天之不可阶而升也。夫子之得邦家者，所谓立之斯立，道之斯行[3]，绥之斯来[4]，动之斯和。其生也荣，其死也哀。如之何其可及也？

【中译文】

陈子禽对子贡说：“您只是表现恭敬罢了，仲尼难道比您更贤能吗？”子贡说：“君子一句话可以证明是明智，一句话也可以证明不明智，所以说话不可不谨慎呀。我们老师的不可超越，就好像天是不能通过阶梯登上去一样。他如能获得治理国家的权位，就会达到这种效果：要百姓安家立业，百姓就会安家立业；要引导百姓，百姓就会跟着走；要安抚百姓，百姓就会来归附；要发动百姓，百姓就会团结协力。他活着很光荣，死了会使人悲哀。我像这样怎么能赶上老师呢？”

【注释】

1 陈子禽：陈亢，字子禽。参阅《学而篇第一》第十章注。

2 知：同“智”。聪明，智慧，明智。

3 道：同“导”。引导。

4 绥（suí）：安抚。

【英译文】

Cheng Ziqin said to Zi Gong, This is an affectation of modesty. The Master is in no way your superior. Zi Gong said, You should be more careful about what you say. A gentleman, though for a single word he may be set down as wise for a single word is set down as a fool. It would be as hard to equal our Master as to climb up on a ladder to the sky. Had our Master ever been put in control of a State or of a great Family, it would have been as is described in the words: 'He raised them, and they stood, he led them and they went. He steadied them as with a rope, and they came. He stirred them, and they moved harmoniously. His life was glorious, his death bewailed.' How can he ever be equalled?

尧曰篇第二十（共三章）

About What Yao Said

20.1

尧曰[1]：“咨[2]！尔舜[3]，天之历数在尔躬[4]，允执其中[5]。四海困穷，天禄永终。”

舜亦以命禹[6]。

曰：“予小子履敢用玄牡[7]，敢昭告于皇皇后帝[8]：有罪不敢赦。帝臣不蔽[9]，简在帝心[10]。朕躬有罪[11]，无以万方；万方有罪，罪在朕躬。”

周有大赉[12]，善人是富。“虽有周亲，不如仁人。百姓有过，在予一人[13]。”

谨权量[14]，审法度[15]，修废官，四方之政行焉。兴灭国，继绝世，举逸民，天下之民归心焉 。

所重：民，食，丧，祭。

宽则得众，信则民任焉[16]，敏则有功，公则说[17]。

【上译文】

尧说：“啊！舜呀！上天的使命落在你身上了，你要诚实地执守中正之道。如果天下百姓陷于贫困，那么上天所赐福禄就会永远终结了。”

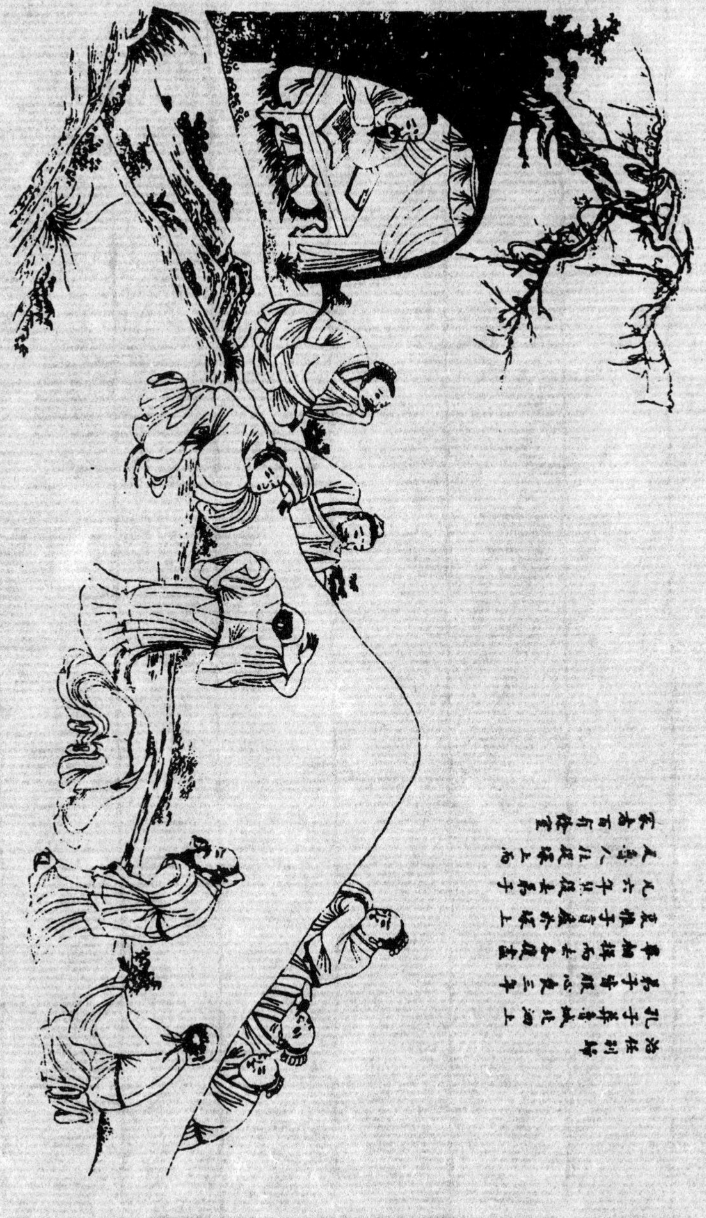

治任别归 Having Fulfilled the Duties and Parting from Each Other

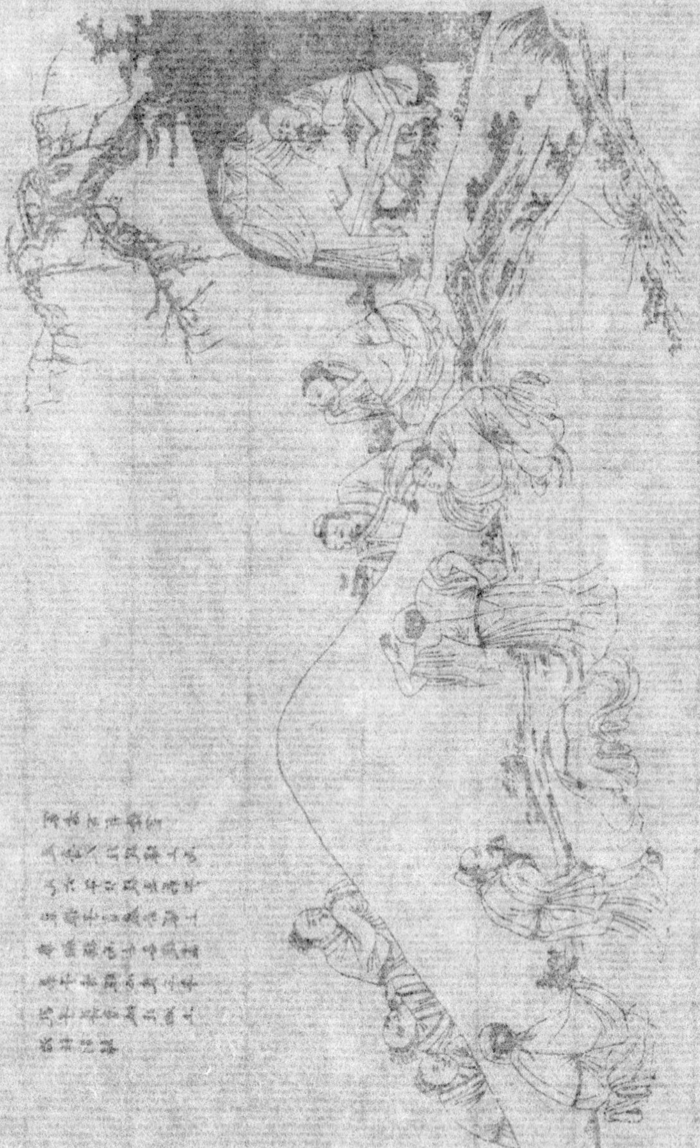

舜也是用这些话告诫禹。

商汤说："我小子履，大胆虔敬地用黑色的公牛来祭祀，向光明而伟大的天帝禀告：对有罪的人，我不敢擅自赦免。您的臣仆的善恶，我也不敢隐瞒掩盖，对此您心里是清楚知道的。如果我自身有罪过，请不要责怪连累天下百姓；天下百姓如果有罪过，都应归在我身上。"

周朝大封诸侯，使善人都得到富贵。周武王说："朕虽有至亲，却不如有仁德的人。百姓如有过错，都应该由我一人来承担。"

谨慎地制定度量衡，检查各种法规制度，恢复被废弃的官职与机构，天下四方的政令就通行了。复兴灭亡了的国家，接续断绝了的世族，推举起用前代被遗落的德才之士，天下民心就归服了。"

国家所要重视的是：人民，粮食，丧葬，祭祀。

做人宽厚，就会得到众人的拥护；诚实守信用，就会得到别人的任用；做事勤敏，就会取得成功；做事公平，就会赢得民心。

【注释】

1 尧：传说中新石器时代我国父系氏族社会后期的部落联盟的领袖。他把君位禅（shàn）让给舜。史称"唐尧"。后被尊称为"圣君"。参阅《泰伯篇第八》第二十章注。

2 咨（zī）：感叹词。犹"啧啧"。咂嘴表示赞叹、赞美。

3 舜：传说中受尧禅位的君主。后来，他又把君位禅让给禹。传说他眼睛有两个瞳仁，又名"重华"。参阅《泰伯篇第八》第二十章注。

4 天之历数：天命。这里指帝王更替的一定次序。古代帝王常常假托天命，都说自己能当帝王是由天命所决定的。

5 允：诚信，公平。执：掌握，保持，执守。中：正，不偏不倚，不"过"也无"不及"。

6 "舜亦"句："禹"，传说中受舜禅位的君主。姒（sì）姓，亦称"大禹"、"夏禹"、"戎禹"，以治水名闻天下。关于舜禅位时嘱咐大禹的话，可参阅《尚书·大禹谟》。

7 予小子履：商汤自称。"予"，我。"小子"，祭天地时自称，表示自己是天帝的儿子（天之子，天子）。"履"，商汤的名字。商汤，历史上又称武汤，武王，天乙，成汤（或成唐），也称高祖乙。他原为商族领袖，任用伊尹执政，积聚力量，陆续攻灭邻近各小国，最后一举灭夏桀，建立了商朝，是孔子所说的"贤王"。敢：谦辞，犹言"冒昧"。含虔诚意。玄牡："玄"，黑色。"牡"，公牛。宰杀后作祭祀用的牺牲。按此段文字又见《尚书·汤诰》，文字略有不同，可参阅。

8 皇皇：大，伟大。后帝："后"，指君主。古代天子和诸侯都称"后"，到了后世，才称帝王的正妻

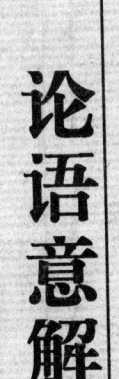

为后。“帝”，古代指最高的天神。这里“后”和“帝”是同一个概念，指天帝。

9 帝臣：天下的一切贤人都是天帝之臣。

10 简：本义是检阅，检查。这里有知道，明白，清楚了解的意思。

11 朕（zhèn）：我。古人不论地位尊卑都自称朕。从秦始皇起，才成为帝王专用的至尊的自称。

12 大赉（lài）：大发赏赐，奖赏百官，分封土地。

13 “虽有”句：“周”，至，最。“百姓”，这里指各族各姓受封的贵族。传说商末就有八百个诸侯。此句又见《尚书·泰誓》，文字略有不同，可参阅。

14 权：秤锤。指计重量的标准。量：量器。指计容积的标准。

15 法度：指计量长度的标准。

16 “信则”句：“民”，疑当作“人”，他人，别人。“任”，任用。诚实守信就会得到他人任用。一说，“民”，百姓。“任”，信任。诚恳守信，就会得到百姓信任。另说，汉代石经等一些版本无此五字，乃《阳货篇第十七》第六章文字而误增于此。

17 说：同“悦”。高兴。本章文字，前后不连贯，疑有脱漏。风格也不同。前半章文字古奥，可能是《论语》的编订者引自当时可见的古代文献。从“谨权量”以下，大多数学者认为可能就是孔子所说的话了。

【英译文】

The Sage King Yao said, "Oh you, Shun! The Heavenly succession now rests upon you. You must faithfully hold fast the correct principles. If the people under Heaven run into poverty, your heavenly gift will be no more."

Zi Zhang asked, "Can you elaborate on these?"

The Master (Confucius) said, "If he gives the people only advantages they deserve, is he not being gracious without extravagance? If he imposes upon them only such tasks as they are capable of performing, is he working them without making them resentful? If a man, out of desire for goodness, achieves it, how can he be said to be greedy? A gentleman, irrespective of whether he iw dealing with many persons or with few, with the small or with the great, never presumes to slight them, is not this indeed being composed without conceit? A gentleman keeps his clothes and hat straight and his glances good-willed; and because of his seriousness, people feel a reverence as they look up at him-isn't this to inspire awe without brutality?"

Zi Zhang asked, "What are the four evils?"

The Master (Confucius) said, "To put men to death without having educated them: this is cruelty. To expect the completion of tasks without giving proper advisement: this is outrageousness. To insist upon punctual completion after the instruction to proceed carefully; this is torment. To promise a reward but to begrudge its payment: this is pettiness."

20.2

子张问于孔子曰：“何如斯可以从政矣[1]？”子曰：“尊五美，屏四恶[2]，斯可以从政矣。”子张曰：“何谓五美？”子曰：“君子惠而不费，劳而不怨，欲而不贪[3]，泰而不骄，威而不猛。”子张曰：“何

庄重威严而不凶猛吗？”子张说：“什么叫四种恶政？”孔子说：“事先不进行教育，犯了错就惩罚，这叫残酷；事先不告诫不打招呼，而要求马上做事成功，这叫粗暴；开始时松懈，却突然限期完成，这叫害人，应当给人东西，拿出手时又不吝啬，这叫算计。”

【注释】

1 斯：就。

2 屏（bǐng）：通“摒”。除去，排除，摈弃。

3 欲而不贪：指其欲在实行仁义，而不在贪图财利。皇侃《论语义疏》：“欲仁义者为廉，欲财色者为贪。”

4 有司：本为官吏的统称。这里指库吏之类的小官，他们在财物出入时都要精确算计。从政的人如果这样，就显得吝啬刻薄而小家子气了。

【英译文】

The Sage King Yao said, "Oh you, Shun! The Heavenly succession now rests upon you. You must faithfully hold fast the correct principles. If the people under Heaven run into poverty, your heavenly gift will be no more."

Zi Zhang asked, "Can you elaborate on these?"

The Master (Confucius) said, "If he gives the people only advantages they deserve, is he not being gracious without extravagance? If he imposes upon them only such tasks as they are capable of performing, is he working them without making them resentful? If a man, out of desire for goodness, achieves it, how can he be said to be greedy? A gentleman, irrespective of whether he iw dealing with many persons or with few, with the small or with the great, never presumes to slight them, is not this indeed being composed without conceit? A

子张曰：“何谓惠而不费？”子曰：“因民之所利而利之，斯不亦惠而不费乎？择可劳而劳之，又谁怨？欲仁而得仁，又焉贪？君子无众寡，无小大，无敢慢，斯不亦泰而不骄乎？君子正其衣冠，尊其瞻视，俨然人望而畏之，斯不亦威而不猛乎？”子张曰：“何谓四恶？”子曰：“不教而杀谓之虐；不戒视成谓之暴；慢令致期谓之贼；犹之与人也，出纳之吝谓之有司[4]。”

【中译文】

子张向孔子请教：“怎样做就可以从政呢？”孔子说：“要尊重五种美德，摒除四种恶政，就可以从政了。”子张说：“什么叫五种美德？”孔子说：“君子使百姓得到好处却不浪费；安排劳役，但劳役强度不使百姓生恨；满足欲望在仁义范围内而不纵容贪婪；安舒矜持，而不骄傲放肆；庄重威严，而不凶猛。”子张说：“怎样能使百姓得到好处，却不浪费呢？”孔子说：“让百姓做对他们有利的事，不就是使百姓得到好处而不浪费吗？选择百姓能干得了的劳役让他去干，谁还怨恨呢？希望实行仁义而得到了仁义，还贪求什么财利呢？君子无论人多人少，势力大势力小，都不敢轻慢，这不就是安舒矜持而不骄傲放肆吗？君子衣冠端正整齐，目光神色都庄重严肃，使人望而敬畏，这不就是

gentleman keeps his clothes and hat straight and his glances good-willed; and because of his seriousness, people feel a reverence as they look up at him-isn't this to inspire awe without brutality?"

Zi Zhang asked, "What are the four evils?"

The Master (Confucius) said, "To put men to death without having educated them: this is cruelty. To expect the completion of tasks without giving proper advisement: this is outrageousness. To insist upon punctual completion after the instruction to proceed carefully; this is torment. To promise a reward but to begrudge its payment: this is pettiness."

20.3

孔子曰：“不知命[1]，无以为君子也；不知礼，无以立也；不知言，无以知人也。”

【中译文】

孔子说：“不懂天命，就无法做君子；不懂礼节，就无法自立；不懂得语言，就无法判断认识他人。”

【注释】

1 命：命运，天命。

【英译文】

The Master (Confucius) said, "He who does not understand the will of Heaven cannot be regarded as a gentleman. He who does not know rites cannot take is stand. He who does not understand words cannot understand others."

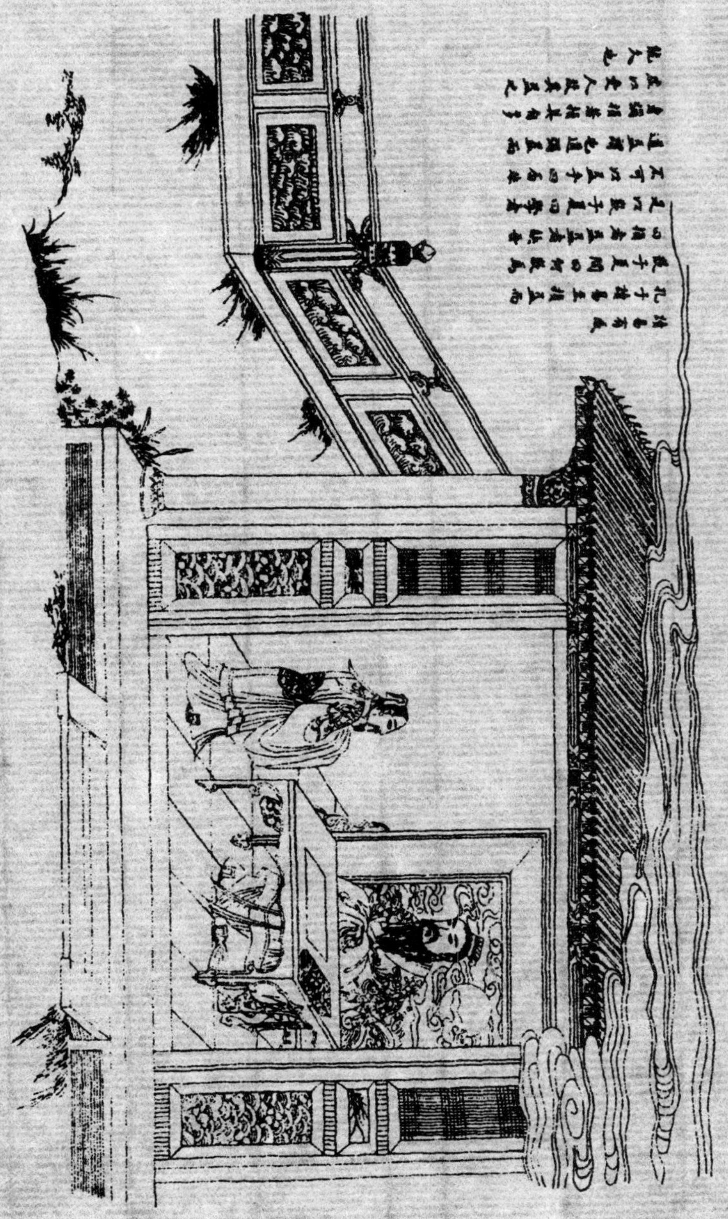

读易有感 The Exclamation after Reading《The Book of Changes》

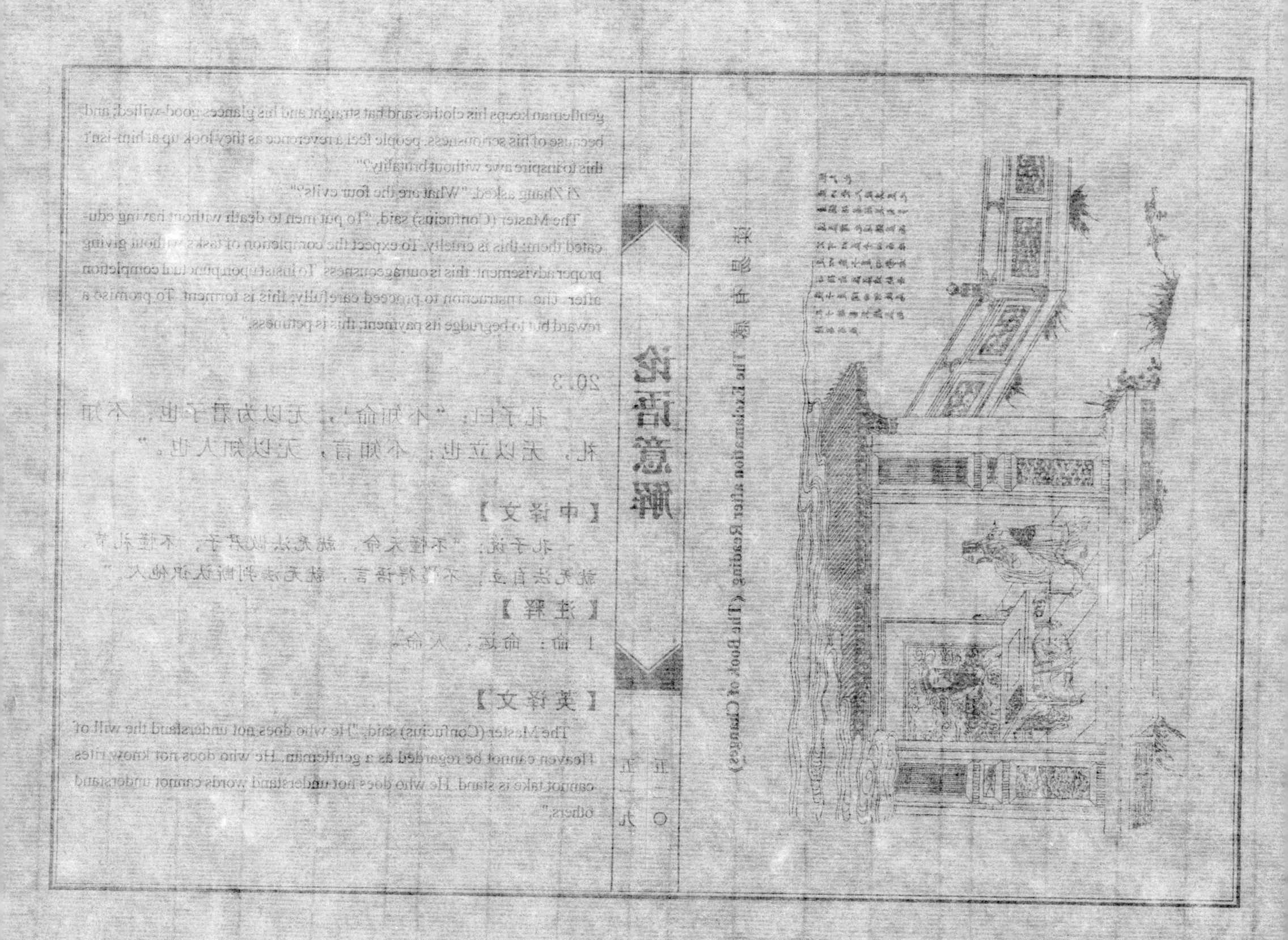

Postscript

This is a very common edition for the Analects of Confucius, which is in the written form of modern Chinese. The reason why it is called The Paraphrase for the Analects is that firstly I think at any rate we can't wholly be in line with the original work; however, we must do our best to conform to the original one. So unavoidably there will be the subjectivity of the interpreter in his interpretation. Secondly differing from the literal interpretation, due to the divergence between the ancient Chinese and the modern Chinese,I more advocate the meaning interpretation.

Hereby I should appreciate Mr. Liyan Li, Mr. tianchen Li and Arthur Waley, the translators of this book from Chinese into English. I am also grateful to the book of The Analects written by Mr, Zhigang Xu, which I comparatively make frequent reference for the annotations during my deciphering . Because of my payiny more emphasis on the significance of the original work as well as the reduction of the possible difference between the original work and the interpretation one due to the view angle of the individual people in modern times, my employment and reference for the annotations are somewhat different . The English titles are translated according to the main contents of the chapters.

Finally I want to say thank you to Ms.LiLi, the editor of the Publishing House of the Thread - bound Books, because it is she whose great kindness helps to bring about this book.

Weijian, liu

Apri15,2005

论语意解

一

后　记

这是一个很普通的《论语》白话版本。之所以叫《论语意解》，是因为我觉得无论如何我们都无法完全回到原作，而又须尽可能地回到原作。这里不可避免地带上了解读者的主观性。其次，与通行的逐字逐句的对译不同，由于古代汉语与现代汉语的差异性，我更主张从意义上进行把握。

在这里要感谢李礼延先生的英译和我在译解过程中注释部分参照较多的人民文学出版社出版的《论语》。由于更注重原作的意义，减少后人的视角所可能形成的导向，我对注释的采用与参照也有所不同。

最后，要感谢线装书局的李莉编辑，是她的盛情与美意促成了我这一自己尚不太满意的劳动。

刘伟见

2005年4月5日